# DEAD ON ICE

*A Lovers in Crime Mystery*

By

Lauren Carr

# DEAD on ICE



For information call: 304-285-8205
or Email: writerlaurencarr@comcast.net



Designed by Acorn Book Services

Publication Managed by Acorn Book Services
www.acornbookservices.com
info@acornbookservices.com
304-285-8205

ISBN-10: 0985726733
ISBN-13: 978-0-9857267-3-7

Printed in the United States of America

*To My Darling Duchess*
*Long Gone, But You Are Always in My Heart*

# DEAD on ICE

## Cast of Characters

*(in order of appearance)*

**Kyle Bostwick:** Angie Sullivan's boyfriend. His last night with her will forever be on his mind.

**Dr. Tad MacMillan:** Chester's home town doctor and Hancock County Medical Examiner. Used to be the town drunk and womanizer. Married to Jan.

**Angelina (Angie) Sullivan:** Eighteen-year-old girl. Disappears June 3, 1978 after leaving Melody Lane Skating Rink in Hookstown, Pennsylvania.

**Brianne Davenport:** Angie Sullivan's best friend. Grows up to own Davenport Winery.

**Cheryl Smith:** Mean girl. Prime suspect in Angie Sullivan's disappearance.

**Ned Carter:** Cheryl Smith's former boyfriend. Grows up to become manager of Mountaineer Resort in Newell, West Virginia.

**Gail Hildebrand:** Friend of Angie Sullivan. Daughter of Mildred and Ralph Hildebrand.

**Doris Sullivan:** Angie's older sister. Owner of Sullivan Stables.

**Albert Gordon:** Criminal Defense Attorney. Elderly widower who lives alone on a small farm in Hookstown, Pennsylvania. Joshua Thornton and Tad MacMillan's distant cousin.

**Joshua Thornton:** Hancock County Prosecuting Attorney. Former JAG lawyer. Widowed father of five. Now his children are growing up and leaving the nest, which allows him the freedom to fall in love with Detective Cameron Gates.

**Detective Cameron Gates:** Pennsylvania State Police Homicide Detective. Joshua Thornton's love interest.

**Irving:** Cameron's Maine Coon cat. Irving has issues, including separation anxiety. You'd have issues, too, if you looked like a skunk.

**Admiral:** Joshua's Irish Wolfhound-Great Dane dog. Irving's friend. His only issue is climbing up onto the furniture when he thinks no one is watching.

**Mildred Hildebrand:** Elderly church lady. Leader and organizer of everything.

**Donny Thornton:** Joshua's youngest son. Sixteen years old. Last baby still left in the nest.

**Jan Martin MacMillan:** Editor of *The Review* newspaper in East Liverpool, Ohio. Tad MacMillan's wife. They're expecting their first baby.

**Ralph Hildebrand:** Mildred Hildebrand's cheating husband.

**Peggy Lawson:** Ralph Hildebrand's office manager and mistress.

**Freddie:** Brianne Davenport's personal assistant.

**Humphrey Phoenix:** Publisher of pornography magazine and movie producer. Discovered Cherry Pickens.

**Detective Harry Shannon**: Original investigator in Angie Sullivan's disappearance.

**Special Investigator William Walton:** FBI Agent with Organized Crime Task Force.

**Randy Vincent:** Cheryl Smith's alibi.

**Mona Vincent:** Randy Vincent's daughter.

**Lieutenant Miles Dugan:** Chief of the homicide division. Detective Cameron Gates' boss.

**Sheriff Curt Sawyer:** Hancock County Sheriff in West Virginia.

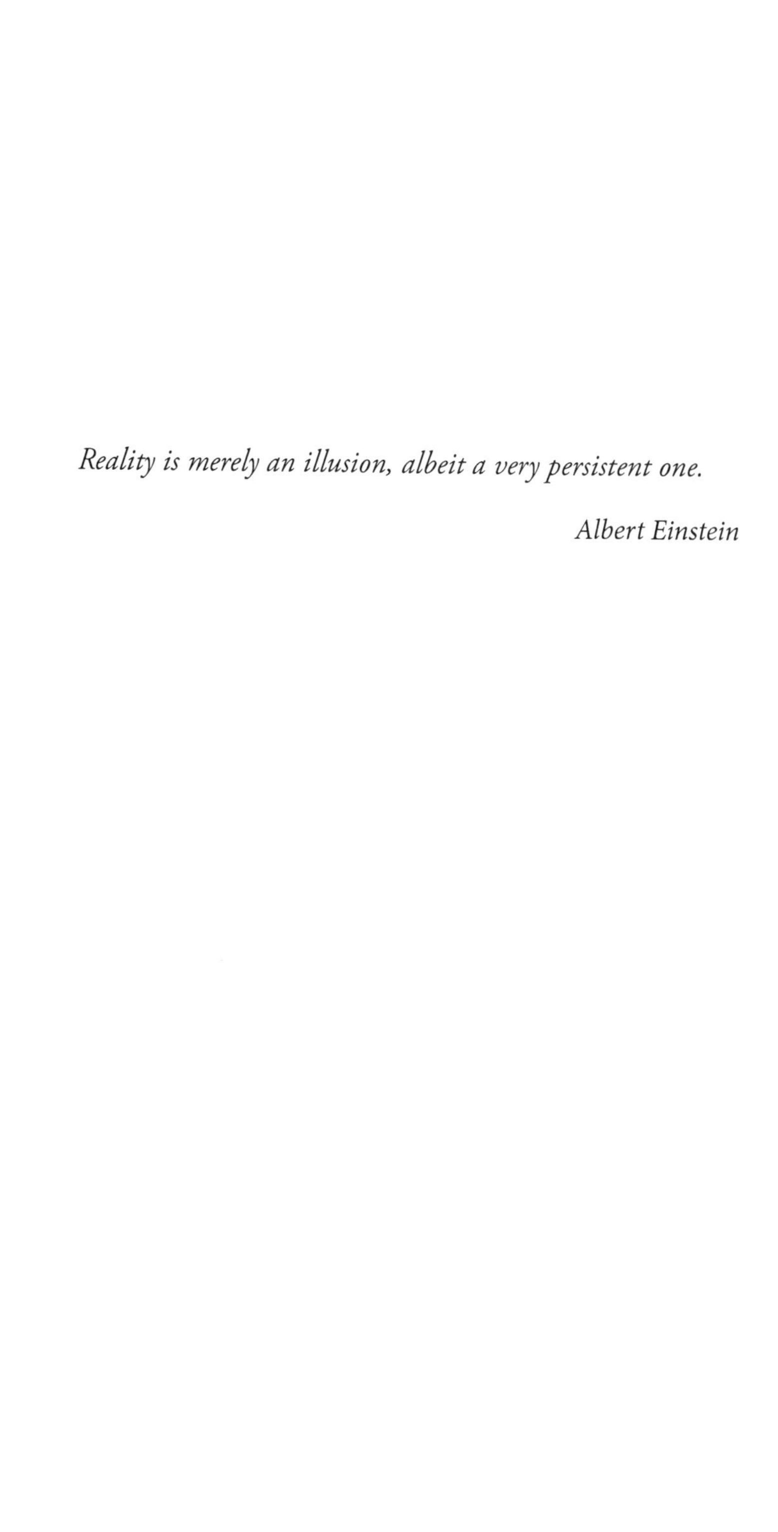

*Reality is merely an illusion, albeit a very persistent one.*

*Albert Einstein*

# DEAD ON ICE

# Prologue

**Saturday Night, June 3, 1978**
**Melody Lane Skating Rink, Hookstown, Pennsylvania**

"For our last slow skate this evening," the announcer's voice boomed over the chatter of the young people filling every corner of the roller skating rink, "we will play 'How Deep Is Your Love' by the Bee Gees."

Situated at the entrance of Hookstown Fairgrounds, Melody Lane Skating Rink was the favorite teenage hangout in the rural towns on either side of the Pennsylvania and West Virginia state line.

The opening notes of the disco tune oozed through the speakers strategically placed in all corners of the rink. Couples who had separated during the course of the evening raced to reconnect in order to cozy up on the dance floor one last time before Melody Lane closed.

Clopping around as if his feet were encased in cement blocks, Kyle Bostwick rubbed his sweaty palms on his blue jeans while craning his neck left to right, and up and down in search of a particular strawberry blonde. He was so anxious in his search that he failed to see the young man with wavy, brown hair making his way onto the rink with a buxom blonde clinging to his arm for balance.

"Whoa." Tad MacMillan clasped his arm to keep him from falling. "Watch where you're going, Kyle. I'd hate to have to run you over for getting in my way."

"Sorry, Tad." Kyle continued his search without concern.

A few years older, Tad had been accepted to West Virginia University School of Medicine, which was quite a surprise to everyone who knew him and even some who didn't. The scandalous party animal had never missed a party in his life. He knew every place in the Ohio Valley to score. "Are you looking for Angie?"

"Yeah, I—"

"I saw her over at the concession with Brianne Davenport." The humor dropped from his face. "She looked really upset."

The blonde was now pulling Tad by both arms out onto the rink.

"What about?" Kyle called over the railing to him.

Captured in a bear hug by the blonde, Tad shrugged before calling over his shoulder. "I heard she had a run-in with Cheryl Smith."

Clinging to the railing, Kyle clomped as fast as his weighted feet could carry him to the other side of the rink and through the doorway to the concession stand. He arrived in time to see Angie's best friend escorting her through what resembled a pack of hyenas yapping and barking jibes in her direction. "Whore! Slut!"

With her white-blond hair cascading into full waves down to her shoulders, Cheryl Smith stood out as the leader of the pack. "You're nothing but a fraud—pretending to be pure as the ivory snow when you're nothing but a whoring bitch."

Angie's hair, the color of strawberries kissed by gold, hung limp in her face. The only friend she seemed to have left in the place had her arms draped around her shoulders. Both girls had turned in their skates and put their shoes back on.

"You have no idea what you're talking about, Cheryl." With her hair falling to her shoulders in one ebony wave, Brianne Davenport was able to dish it back. "You're the bitch for spreading lies."

"I know exactly what I'm talking about," Cheryl sneered. "She's a slutty bitch like her mother. That's where she gets it." She tried to push past Brianne to get into Angie's face. "Teach you to screw around with my boyfriend."

"I never screwed around with Ned," Angie said in her defense. "Whoever told you that was lying."

Kyle rushed in to defend his date. "Leave her alone."

"What are you going to do if I don't?"

When Cheryl lunged at him, Kyle jumped back so fast that he lost his balance. Waving both arms in a vain effort to stay on his feet, he resembled a bird trying to take flight; which caused the pack of hyenas to squeal with laughter.

They continued to deliver cutting comments while Angie and Brianne struggled to help him to his feet. Humiliated by his failed attempt to defend his girl and the continued abuse after his fall, he gave up on the skates. With Angie's help, he untied the laces and kicked them off.

"What a man!" Cheryl's voice dripped with sarcasm as she bent over the three of them.

"What a bitch!" a strong voice retorted.

Seeing another challenge, Cheryl rose up to her height.

The pack backed off at the sight of her estranged boyfriend, Ned Carter, stepping into the room.

"I thought we graduated from school last month," Ned said. "Don't you think it's time to cast aside these schoolgirl games?"

"Like you cast me aside?"

With his wavy-blond hair and chiseled chest, Ned was the motive for her revenge. "Exactly."

"You're not even going to deny it." There was a hint of pain in her anger.

"Nope." He turned to Angie, Kyle, and Brianne. "Time to blow this joint."

"I'm not through with you, Angie!" Cheryl called after them.

❧ ❧ ❧ ❧

*Damn it! This is not at all the way I had planned it—Not at all.*

Caught in the stampede of customers turning in their skates, Kyle lost sight of his date once again. Nervously, he fingered the small felt box in his pants pocket.

There was no need to worry over that. After all, they had come to the skating rink together in her car.

*All is not lost. Since Plan A didn't work out, we'll go for Plan B. We'll stop at the river on our way home. Our place. Yes, that will be even better. I'll ask her when we're alone.*

Outside, he found Ned and Brianne still comforting Angie.

"Would you like us to drive you home?" Brianne asked.

"That's okay," Kyle yelled while jogging across the gravel parking lot in his sock feet. He hopped on one foot while slipping on his loafers. "I'll take care of Angie."

Brianne cast an eye at her.

Angie nodded her head.

The exchange between the friends was broken when another girl who had come out of the skating rink stepped between them. "I just wanted to give you a hug," Gail Hildebrand said in a teary voice. Hugging the girl with a voluptuous figure was like hugging a soft lovable teddy bear.

"Nothing Cheryl said about you and your mom is true. I don't believe it one bit." The white roller skates hanging from her shoulder by the laces swung to hit Kyle in the arm.

Angie hung her head to hide the tears rolling down her cheeks.

When the two girls hugged again, their reddish-blond locks blended to give the appearance of one mane. "I love you, Angie." Even though the teenaged girl was a couple of years younger than those in the group, the strength in her words held a tone of maturity beyond her years.

"Me, too."

They clung to each other's hands when Gail pulled away to go rejoin her friends piling into a car on the other side of the parking lot.

"How about if we come home with you?" Brianne offered again.

"Angie and I have plans," Kyle insisted.

"Are you sure?" Ned asked. "After what happened, I don't think you should be alone tonight."

"She won't be alone," Kyle said. "She'll be with me."

"Cheryl's ruthless," Ned warned them. "If she says she's not through, then she isn't."

Angie shrugged her shoulders and forced a smile across her trembling lips. "School's out, and it's a whole new world—there's more to life than South Side High School and Cheryl's scores to settle. I just don't know where she got the idea that I was fooling around with you, Ned."

"Me, neither." Brianne flipped her black locks back over her shoulder. "Who knows where Cheryl comes up with these crazy ideas? But, as right as you may be, that's not going to be any comfort if she or her friends corner you again."

Ned rested his hand on the door handle. "Maybe I should—"

Wiping Ned's hand off the door handle, Kyle slipped

in-between them and his date. He wrapped his arm around her shoulders. "I'll take care of Angie."

She responded by wrapping her arm around his waist. Her kiss warmed his face. "That's right. You've always been my best friend—through good times and bad, thick and thin."

He added, "Better or worse … richer or poorer."

Brianne and Ned cast glances in each other's directions before stepping back to allow Kyle to open the car door for her.

Ned waited until they were pulling out of the parking lot before slipping his arm around Brianne. "Who would have guessed?"

Sucking in her breath, Brianne clasped his arm when she saw Cheryl's old Camaro pull out onto Main Street to fall in behind Angie's Mustang.

**Next Morning**

"Angie, we're going to be late for church." Doris Sullivan dabbed an extra layer of makeup under her eyes where she saw a new wrinkle appear. Standing up straight, she studied her gaunt features in the bathroom mirror. *Who are you trying to kid, Doris? You're a farmer, not a glamour puss. Hang it up.*

As if in agreement with her assessment, a horse whinnied from out in the pasture. She cast a grin out the window at the half-dozen Thoroughbreds grazing in the field of her horse farm.

*Nope, you weren't a bathing beauty when you were seventeen years old, and you're not one now that you're thirty-five.*

After putting a touch of lipstick onto her lips, she tossed the stick into her purse and stepped out into the hallway. "Angie, wake up." She tapped on the bedroom door on her way to the staircase. "We're going to be late."

When the phone rang downstairs in the living room, she quickened her pace.

"Hello, Mrs. Sullivan," Kyle Bostwick greeted her across the line. "Is Angie up yet? I wanted to say good morning."

"No," she replied, "she's not up yet. How late were you two out last night? She still wasn't home when I went to sleep."

"We were out late."

She didn't like the chuckle that came across the line. "How late?"

There was silence at the other end of the line before Kyle said, "I'll let her tell you what happened last night."

Concerned by the tone of his voice, and that it was something that Kyle didn't want to tell her himself, Doris put down the phone and climbed the stairs to Angie's room. When there was no reply to her knock, she opened the door.

Her hands flew to her mouth as if to catch her heart threatening to leap up out of her throat when she saw that the bed had not been slept in.

Angelina Sullivan was missing.

# CHAPTER ONE

**Present Day**
**Hancock County Courthouse**
**New Cumberland, West Virginia**

"Your honor, at this time, the defense would like to request that the charges against my client for driving while under the influence be dismissed." Albert Gordon reached up to present a report to the judge and stepped over to the prosecution table to hand a copy to the prosecuting attorney, Joshua Thornton. "As evidenced by this report, you will find that the Breathalyzer that the officer had used to conduct the test on my client was sent for repairs the very day after the defendant was arrested. If the machine was defective, then this calls into question the validity of the evidence against my client."

Trying not to frown, Joshua read the information he held in his hands.

The facts were before him in black and white. The same machine used to gauge the blood alcohol level of the young man sitting at the defense table had been sent in for repairs hours later.

*This is not good.*

When he cast a sidelong glance at the arresting officer, Joshua saw the sheriff deputy's cheeks redden before he looked down at his hands in his lap.

Brad Hendrix had already been convicted twice for driving while under the influence. This time, a nursing student was seriously injured when he rammed his truck into her car. Prosecutor Joshua Thornton wanted this third conviction. He wanted this mandatory jail time. Most importantly, Joshua wanted Hendrix off the roads before he killed someone.

Albert Gordon's illustrious career as a defense attorney had made him a legend in the tri-state area. Joshua had only to imagine how his distant cousin, Albert, had managed to learn about the machine's malfunction that warranted it being repaired after Brad Hendrix's arrest.

The judge took off her glasses. "Mr. Thornton, I'll hear your objections now."

"Your honor," Joshua said, "the Breathalyzer was used after the police pulled the defendant out of the lake in which he had driven his truck—after driving it off the road and across three back yards while evading arrest. This is his third arrest for driving while under the influence—"

"Objection," Albert shouted.

Before the judge could sustain the objection, Joshua apologized for raising Hendrix's past convictions. Albert had them excluded from the evidence. "Your honor, the defendant was driving recklessly. He's a hazard and—"

"Your honor," Albert interjected, "the fact is that the Breathalyzer would never have gone in for repair if it had been working properly, in which case the arresting officers shouldn't have used it, and the results should never have been entered into evidence. The reading from that test is inadmissible, and without a proper gauge of my client's alcohol content, then the charge should be dropped."

"Mr. Gordon is right," the judge said to Joshua. "The DUI charge is dropped."

Joshua tried to not look in the direction of the defendant's table. He was afraid that he'd slap Hendrix's smirk right off his face.

The judge continued, "But the charges of speeding, reckless driving, and avoiding arrest will remain." She went on to set the trial to start the next week and adjourn the hearing.

While packing up his briefcase, Joshua saw Albert say something to his client that made the young man stomp his feet and slam his fist down on the table. After spouting a curse at the man who had gotten him off for what would have been a certain conviction and jail time, he hurried out of the courtroom.

"Congratulations, counselor," Joshua greeted Albert when he crossed the aisle. "Your client isn't out of hot water yet."

"That's what I told him. Why do you think he was so happy when he left?" Albert's expression was not that of a man who had won a pre-trial motion. He ran his hand, which was covered with age spots, over his suit's lapel. "Can we talk?"

"Isn't that what we're doing?"

"About a deal."

Joshua wondered why he had never noticed it before. He had known Albert his whole life, but for the first time he realized how much his cousin had aged. Even though he was one of the most respected defense attorney's in the area, which enabled him to afford practically the best of anything; his suit was faded and wrinkled. He was stooped over. Judging by the lack of sparkle in his manner, Joshua suspected he didn't care enough to exert the effort into standing up straight.

Joshua slung his valise across his shoulder. "What kind of deal, Al?"

"You and I both know that jail isn't what Brad needs. He's a drunk. He needs rehab."

"The first step in that is admitting he has a problem. He thinks he's all right. You can see that by how he blames everyone else for his accidents and arrests. The rest of the world is the one with a problem. He's right. We do have a problem." Joshua jerked a thumb toward the door. "Anyone who is out on the road after he's tied one on has a problem."

Albert nodded his head in agreement. "You know that I don't make a habit of defending DUI's. The only reason I've been dealing with Brad is because his mother begged me to keep him out of jail."

"So she's an enabler."

"She's his mother. You'd be the same way if it was one of your kids."

"I have no problem with tough love. It did a lot for me."

Albert let out a heavy breath. "Will you listen to my offer?"

Joshua sat on the corner of the counsel table and folded his arms across his chest. "I'm listening."

Albert leaned against the railing separating the court from the gallery where the spectators sat. "We get a continuance for the trial. Brad goes into rehab for thirty days. He stays the whole thirty days and you drop the charges."

Joshua laughed. "What if it doesn't take? What if he lea—"

"You stipulate that as part of the agreement. If he skips out, the trial goes on. I plead him guilty, and he goes to jail for whatever time *you* recommend."

"What if he stays and as soon as I drop the charges, he takes up where he left off?"

"You can get a continuance for up to a year," Albert said. "That's part of the agreement. We agree to random drug tests. If he flunks a drug test, or gets into *any* trouble, then he pleads guilty to these charges, and it's off to jail." He jerked his thumb over his shoulder. "Hendrix has to remain clean and sober, and on the straight and narrow, for a year before you drop the charges."

Joshua hesitated. If it was any other lawyer he would have said hogwash, but Albert Gordon was family.

Albert was the son of his grandmother's sister. As a child, Joshua Thornton recalled sitting next to his great-aunt in court and watching Albert up front working his cases. He introduced Joshua to the world of law and inspired him to be a lawyer like him—a soldier for justice.

Joshua's thoughts were interrupted by the opening of the door at the back of the otherwise deserted courtroom.

"Hey you!"

A wide smile crossed Joshua's face at the sight of Cameron Gates.

Albert turned to the approaching woman clad in black slacks and leather jacket over a white turtleneck. Her semi-automatic Colt handgun and Pennsylvania State Police shield were displayed on her belt. Her wavy, short, dark hair fell down to her eyebrows and over the collar of her sweater.

In her arms, she carried what appeared to be a large skunk on a leather leash.

The intrusion on their discussion caused Albert to stand up. "This must be the lady I've been hearing so much about." He reached out to stroke the black Maine Coon cat with the white stripe down his back from the top of his head to the tip his bushy tail. Tuffs of white fur stuck out of his black ears. "And this must be Irving, the infamous skunk cat."

"If they're talking about a lady, they must be talking about someone else." While cradling the cat in one arm, she reached out to grasp Joshua by the back of the neck and kiss him.

Slipping his arm across her shoulders, Joshua introduced her to Albert. "Cameron and I have been seeing each other since this past summer. She's a homicide detective with the Pennsylvania State Police."

"Is Irving her partner?" Albert joked. "I've heard of K-9, do they have feline patrols now?"

"Quasi," she replied. "He loves to ride in the cruiser with me. I've finally gotten him to the point of spending the day with Joshua when he works at home. Irving likes Admiral."

Albert looked over at Joshua, who was nodding his head. "Your Irish Wolfhound?"

"They're good buddies," Joshua said. "Irving hates me."

As if to demonstrate his agreement, the cat narrowed his emerald green eyes and let out a growl deep in his throat while glaring at Joshua.

"Irving has issues," Cameron said.

"Irving's crazy," Joshua clarified.

"Which is an issue."

"Pennsylvania?" Albert led her back to the subject of her status as a homicide detective. "Is Hookstown part of your jurisdiction?"

After she told him that it was, she asked in a teasing tone, "Have you killed anyone there?"

"I live on a little farm out in Hookstown," Albert told her. "Snowden Road. Actually, it's not really a farm anymore. I don't have any livestock … since my wife passed away almost thirty years ago." His voice trailed off while a distant look came to his eyes.

An awkward silence filled the courtroom. Joshua tightened his grip on Cameron's shoulder. Uttering a meow, Irving reached out a paw to touch Albert's arm.

With a smile, the elderly man patted the top of the cat's head. "Yes, we had quite a few cats in that old barn. Great mousers those cats were." Abruptly, he told them, "I need to get going. I'm late for an appointment." He shook Joshua's hand. "I'll call you later about that deal."

He rushed down the aisle to the courtroom doors before stopping. "You have been very blessed, Joshua. Not every man gets a second shot at love after burying his wife. I hope you realize that." Before they could respond, he hurried out and was gone.

"What was that about?" Cameron asked after the clang of the courtroom doors shutting had quieted.

Joshua shrugged his shoulders. "Albert never got over his wife dying back all those years ago. Eventually, he sold all of the livestock on his farm, and now, he lives there alone. All he's got is the house and his legal practice."

With his arm across her shoulders, they walked down the aisle toward the door.

"Is he any good … as a lawyer?"

"He's very good. He beat my butt today." Joshua stopped at the door. "He goes to my church. I see him every Sunday. But today, it was like I actually looked at him for the first time. I never noticed how old he was."

"We're all getting older." She brushed her fingers through his silver hair. "I've seen the pictures of you back when you were in JAG," she smiled. "Your hair was darker then. But I like it better now. I love my silver fox."

"I've earned every one of these silver locks." He pointed to his head. "Let's lock you up in a house with five teenagers and see how long your hair remains cinnamon-colored."

"Am I allowed to stay armed?"

"I was armed, and it didn't do me any good."

"That's why I have a cat instead of children." Keeping hold of his leash, she put Irving down. "Albert's aged. It happens to all of us eventually."

"But, it's like he's aged twenty years overnight. I think I'm going to invite him to dinner after church this Sunday."

Instead of responding, she was watching Irving wrap his leash around Joshua's leg.

"Do you mind?" he asked while stepping out of the confines of the leash.

"It's your house." She picked up the cat before he had a chance to tie Joshua up again. "You can have whoever you want."

"You think he's weird."

"I didn't say your cousin was weird," she said.

"You didn't have to. I could see it on your face."

She squinted at him. "I have a poker face, I'll have you know. That's why I'm so good at interrogation. No one knows what I'm thinking *ever*."

"If you say so." Joshua went through the door.

"I do say so." She followed him. "Just for that, you're buying me a pizza with everything on it."

"How about a bacon cheeseburger and waffle fries?"

"I'm easy. I'll settle for that. Remember, non-fat milk for Irving. He's watching his weight."

Irving agreed with a meow.

~ ~ ~ ~

Albert Gordon never missed Sunday service at the First Christian Church on Indiana Avenue in Chester. There was no sign on the left aisle seat in the third pew back, but it was understood that was Albert's seat. That's why everyone noticed when he wasn't there the next Sunday.

Joshua Thornton and his family sat directly across the aisle from Albert. Over the years, as four of Joshua's five children had flown the nest, the crowd that filled the pew was reduced down to that of father and his youngest son.

Oldest sons, Murphy had graduated from the Naval Academy and his twin, Joshua Junior from pre-law at Pennsylvania State University. Murphy was now serving at the Pentagon while J.J. was embarking on law school. Younger daughter, Sarah had taken Murphy's place at the Naval Academy in Annapolis; while her older sister Tracy was with the CIA; Culinary Institute of America, that is. The only junior Thornton left was Donny, who was a sophomore at Oak Glen High School.

The baby of the family was no more. As if in response to his siblings' teasing for being the runt of the family, Donny hit puberty with style by sprouting over a foot between twelve and thirteen years of age. At sixteen, he was two inches taller than both his father and brothers.

Rebelling at first to his father's insistence that he go out for football to get him away from his computers and into the fresh air; Donny discovered that he had inherited his father's talent for football. In his youth, Joshua had led his high school to the state championship. Whoever would have guessed Joshua's computer geek son would become a top linebacker?

The exercise served Donny well. As much as he hated to admit his father was right, he was pleased to discover that his toned muscles gave him a physique to complement the Thornton dark, wavy hair and striking blue eyes. He had no trouble getting dates on Friday and Saturday nights, which made for less time with his computer games, which made Joshua happy.

Several years since returning to Chester after the death of his wife had left him with five children to raise on his own, Joshua found that he would still do a double-take when Dr. Tad MacMillan, stepped up onto the stage behind the church pastor to lead the choir. If ever there was proof that people can change, it was his cousin.

A little over ten years ago, Tad MacMillan was a womanizing town drunk. Rumor was that the charismatic rogue had slept with every available woman in the Ohio Valley. Now, he was Chester's town doctor and Hancock County's medical examiner. At an age when most people were becoming grandparents, Tad and his wife, Jan, were expecting their first baby.

"Is Albert sick?" Mildred Hildebrand blocked Joshua's exit out the front door after the service. Her tone was not unlike that of a boss wanting to know where one of her employees had disappeared.

Mildred went to great lengths to dress for her role of church leader in colorful suits, scarves, and hats. While most of the congregation had bundled up in heavy sweaters and winter boots to defend themselves against January's freezing winds, Mildred donned a winter ensemble, which included a wide-brimmed, red hat trimmed in white fur.

Joshua cocked his head to look beyond her hat to see Donny engaged in a conversation with a pretty girl with long blond hair. Her family was new to their church, and the young man had swooped in as soon as the service was over to introduce himself.

"When are we going to meet your new lady friend?" Mildred went on to demand. "She does go to church, doesn't she? Donny needs a mother who will reinforce his religious upbringing."

"Cameron is Catholic. She goes to Mass every Saturday at St. George's in Aliquippa."

When Joshua tried to sidestep her to catch Donny's attention, Mildred sidestepped with him.

When he saw his father trying to catch his eye, Donny turned his head. The blond was smiling up at him.

Another one of Albert's elderly friends Doris Sullivan grasped Joshua's elbow from behind. The tall, gaunt woman's cold, bony fingers felt like bird claws gripping his arm, which caused him to let out a shriek at her unexpected touch.

"I hope Albert isn't sick," she said. "Now that I think about it, I haven't seen his car move out of his driveway in days." Doris Sullivan lived alone on a horse farm located along the same country road. The Sullivan family bred and raced Thoroughbred horses. After giving up the livestock on his farm, Albert allowed Doris' horses to graze in his fields.

"He must be," Joshua said. "He was in court the other day, and he wasn't feeling well."

"He didn't come to the spaghetti dinner Friday night." Mildred crossed her hands and rested them on her plump tummy. "Albert always comes to our spaghetti dinners, or any functions the church has that offers a meal."

Her displeased expression made Joshua feel as if he had done something wrong. He resisted the urge to tell her that it wasn't his job to watch his elderly, distant cousin. He noticed Ralph Hildebrand, Mildred's husband, make a gesture at Doris from behind his wife's back and slip out the front door into the wind.

"He says he likes our cooking," Doris said. "Excuse me." With a quick glance over her shoulder to see that Joshua still had Mildred's attention, she followed Ralph out the front door.

The reference to their good cooking brought a smile to Mildred's face. "Albert loves my coconut cream pie." She glanced both ways before telling Joshua in a low tone, "Doris baked a cake for our Thanksgiving dinner. Albert told me that he had to sneak it into the garbage. It was so bad." With a laugh, she looked over across the back of the sanctuary in search of her rival.

Refusing to join in the gossip, Joshua finally caught Donny's eye and excused himself.

"Should I stop by Albert's house to check on him?" Mildred called after him.

"No," Joshua replied while hurrying away. "I'll do it. He's my family."

Grabbing Donny by the arm, he led him outside. "Haven't I told you that when Mrs. Hildebrand starts talking to me to come tell me that you want to go home?"

"That was Sarah's job," Donny said.

"Now that she's gone, you've inherited it."

"Man! Irving, you're so lucky you have that nice fur coat." Cameron waited for the gust of wind to pass before pulling up the collar on her winter coat and throwing open her SUV's door. The wind whipped her hair around her head while she ran up the sidewalk to the front porch of the farmhouse on Snowden Road.

Catching a whiff of the freezing wind during the brief moment the door was open, Irving backed up to his seat on the passenger side of the car and curled up under the blower where the hot air had been coming out of the heater.

Cameron had checked Albert's mail and paper boxes at the end of his long driveway. She counted four newspapers in his box, and the mailbox was full of bills and advertisements.

Deduction: He hadn't collected his mail or newspapers for several days.

After noting that the elderly man's sidewalk and porch were still clear of snow from his shoveling it following the blizzard the week before, she pounded on the front door. "Mr. Gordon!" she yelled. "Mr. Gordon! It's Detective Cameron Gates, Joshua's friend. Are you okay? Your family has asked me to check on you! Can you answer the door?"

The only movement was Irving's head popping up to peer at her from the driver's side window of the car. His meow sounded like an order to hurry up.

"I'll be there in a minute," she replied. "Keep your tail on."

Irving returned to the passenger seat to wait.

She went around to the side door that opened to a breezeway leading into the kitchen. The lock was old and would be a piece of cake for her to pick. She reached into the inside breast pocket of her coat and extracted her lock pick kit. After glancing around to determine that no one was around to watch, she knelt to get to work. Unable to feel the inside workings of the pick in the lock, she was forced to take off her gloves. Her fingertips instantly went numb. The wind went down her neck to send a shiver through her body.

*The things I do for my friends.*

"Careful. Someone watching might think you were breaking and entering."

Startled, she whirled around so fast that she lost her balance and landed on her rump in a pile of snow. Joshua's and Donny's laughter could have been heard across the snow covered acres around them.

"What are you doing here?" she asked.

"Checking on Albert," Joshua said. "What are you doing?"

"Tad called and asked me to stop by on my way to your place," she said. "Seems Albert wasn't in church." She returned to picking the lock. "I don't suppose you have a key to any of these locks."

After saying he didn't, Joshua poked around under the door mat and other places he could think of where Albert would hide a key to use in case he locked himself out of his home.

"There are four newspapers in his paper box," she told them. "Everything is locked up tight. We have to break in."

"He's either out of town, or something happened to him," Donny said.

"And leave his car behind?" She pointed to the car parked in front of the garage.

"Why didn't he park it in the garage?" Joshua asked.

"Probably not enough room." She peered into the lock while working the pick. "The garage looks like it's filled with junk. Take a look in the window."

"Maybe someone drove him to the airport." Hugging himself, Donny stomped his feet to keep warm.

Joshua shook his head. "Albert is one of those people who thinks that if you go beyond Pittsburgh that you're going to drop off the ends of the earth. He doesn't go out except for court, church functions, and Sunday services."

Donny peered through the kitchen window as if it were possible to see through the thick curtains blocking the view inside. "If we break in and he went to Vegas for a vacation, then we'll be charged with breaking and entering."

Her hand on the door knob, Cameron stood up. "You know, it's surprising how easy it is to pick these old locks. We'll simply open the door. Step inside to make sure Albert is okay. If he's not here and hurt, then we can leave and lock the door behind us, and no one will even know we were here."

She pushed open the door and went inside. Her scream brought Joshua and Donny in at a run. None of them had ever seen a scene like that stretched out before them.

Floor-to-ceiling, wall-to-wall; the house was packed with everything that had ever come through the doors: mail (both opened and unopened), church bulletins, newsletters, gifts still in their boxes, clothes, cushions, books, magazines, blankets, games, newspapers, and anything else imaginable. If it had ended up in Albert Gordon's possession, it didn't leave his home.

The side door opened into what was designed to be the dining room. An unused fireplace with a brick mantle filled the far wall. The space inside the fireplace was filled up to the chimney with magazines. The mantle itself contained stacks of papers. On the other side of the room, an archway opened into the living room.

"Oh, my God," Donny breathed. "It looks like a junk shop."

"More like a dump." Regaining her composure, Cameron noticed a sickening odor. It was unmistakable. She had smelled it before at crime scenes of victims who had died and started decomposing.

Covering his face to block out the smell, Joshua picked his way through a path that Albert had cut through over the years. "Now we know why he never invited anyone to his house. I remember coming here when I was a kid. This must have happened after his wife passed away."

Cameron took a different path through the living room to search for the source of the odor. She covered her face with her hand to cut off the sickening smell, but it didn't help. In case of the worst scenario, she made sure not to touch anything for fear of contaminating possible evidence. She turned on the overhead light in the living room.

Joshua turned on the foyer light.

As soon as light flooded the foyer he saw it.

It was a hand sticking out from under a mountain of yellowed newspapers. The flesh on the appendage was bloated and cracked.

Albert Gordon's body was in advance stages of decomposition.

# Chapter Two

**One Week Later**

"You're not the boss of me, Mildred Hildebrand."

Upon arriving at Albert Gordon's home, Doris Sullivan wasted no time in announcing that she had come to help pack up the dearly departed man's belongings; but wasn't taking orders from anyone. With that said, she clutched her oversized handbag under her arm and scurried down to the cellar to begin working from the ground up.

Having no children, Albert had left his entire estate to the church. Totaling over a quarter of a million dollars, his sizable bank accounts would prove to be a big financial relief for the church.

His farm proved not to be such a blessing.

It was only upon his death that Albert Gordon's family and friends discovered the depth of the wound inflicted by his wife's passing. They could only conclude that between grief and depression, or possibly his inability to care for his home; Albert had let things get out of hand. Every building on the

Gordon property was packed with junk, which had ended up killing the elderly man.

Autopsy and forensics investigation revealed that Albert had suffered a stroke from which he could have survived. However, when he had collapsed on the stairs in his home, the newspapers that lined the stairway fell on top of him to smother him to death.

Doris Sullivan immediately offered to buy the farmland and house—lock-stock-and-barrel. Even after Joshua and his cousin Tad had given her a tour of the farmhouse to show her the extent of her neighbor's hoarding, she insisted on wanting the property as-is to combine with her Sullivan Stables.

That seemed like a dream come true to Joshua, the executor of the estate. Unloading a hoarder property at the asking price is unheard of in real estate.

Unfortunately, Tad MacMillan would have none of it. He refused to let Joshua accept any offer until every building on Albert's farm was cleaned out and any possible family memorabilia confiscated.

Simply thinking about it gave Joshua a headache.

In an effort to save as much money in the estate as possible, the church ladies got together and volunteered to clean out Albert's house so that it could be sold.

Joshua suspected Mildred didn't want to help as much as she was anxious to stick her nose into Albert's business and go through his stuff. To keep a leash on her, Joshua dragged Donny out of bed to go help out.

Cameron jumped out of bed after a late night staking out the apartment of a murder suspect's girlfriend. Usually, she would be barely functional after only four hours sleep, but her persistence had proven successful. The detective had managed to nab her man when he tried to give the cops the slip by sneaking into the apartment through the fire escape at two o'clock in the morning.

With the thrill of victory coursing through her veins, Cameron arrived at the farm to join Joshua, Donny, Tad, and Jan in hauling furniture out of the house to be carted off either to the dump or an estate dealer who had agreed to take it.

Wanting to ensure there was no misunderstanding about who was in charge, Mildred Hildebrand was at Albert's home at the crack of dawn. Dressed in a khaki pant suit accented with sparkling beads in a floral pattern, she stood out as the manager of the cleanup operation. Upon each volunteer's arrival, she greeted him or her with a clipboard clutched to her chest to hand out his or her assignment.

After Doris rebuffed Mildred's orders, Joshua went into the kitchen for another dose of coffee where he found Irving perched on the kitchen counter. The cat's long tail twitched while he glared at the basement doorway through which the renegade volunteer had just stormed to go downstairs.

"I'm glad to see that you've found someone else to glare at." Joshua scratched the top of the skunk cat's head. Irving shook his head and batted at his ear as if to erase Joshua's touch before returning his attention toward the basement doorway.

"There must be mice downstairs," Cameron said while holding open a garbage bag for Jan MacMillan to toss old cans and boxes from the cupboard.

A low growl built up from deep in Irving's throat. His tail continued twitching.

"Go get 'em, if you smell mice," Joshua told him.

Irving skimmed the edge of the kitchen counter, which was the only space clear of cans and boxes emptied from the cupboard. Once he reached where his mistress was holding the garbage bag, he sat down and twitched his tail while staring at her.

"I'm surprised to see Doris Sullivan here," Jan said.

"She and Albert have been neighbors almost their whole lives," Joshua said. "He had let her horses graze in his fields all these years, and she's offering to buy the farm. The sooner this place is cleaned out, the sooner we can close the deal."

Cameron asked, "What's she going to do with the house?"

"Renovate it and then rent it out," Joshua said. "Maybe even sell it. The main thing she wants is the land to expand her horse farm."

"My point is that I've never seen Doris volunteer for anything like this," Jan said. "I guess you're right. She does have an interest in getting this place cleaned out so that she can buy it." She patted her bulging tummy. "Hormones are making me suspicious."

The bag full, Cameron tied it shut and held it out to Joshua to drag outside. When he didn't move to take the bag in response to her silent order, she flashed him a seductive look that included an arched eyebrow. A slow grin crossed his face before he took the bag.

After she was alone with Jan, Cameron whispered, "Man, Mrs. Hildebrand sure is bossy."

"If she tells me one more time that I've got a glow about me, I'm going to tape her mouth shut." When she saw Cameron cocking her head at her, she apologized, "Sorry, hormones make me cranky, too."

"I have duct tape in the trunk of my car. I'll let you have the whole roll. It's right next to my bullet-proof vest."

"You carry duct tape in your trunk?" Jan asked.

"You never know when you're going to need to restrain someone."

A high-pitched scream erupted from behind them. Cameron grabbed for her gun only to remember she wasn't wearing it on her belt.

"Skunk!" Dropping a cooler to the floor, a man blocked the screaming woman with his body while pointing at the cat on the counter.

Irving jumped down from the counter and ran from the kitchen while the screaming couple looked for cover.

"That's not a skunk. That's a cat," Cameron yelled over the hysteria. "You two need to grow some guts."

"Cat?" the woman replied. "Are you sure? I ain't never seen a cat that looked like that before. He's so big."

When the woman stepped out from behind her protector, Cameron saw that she was a middle-aged voluptuous blonde. Twenty or so years ago, she had probably been a bombshell. With the passage of time and refusal to age gracefully, she had morphed from beauty to sideshow attraction. Her hair was twice as big as her head, and her red sweater had a plunging neckline to reveal sagging breasts. Brightly colored rouge and lipstick, thick mascara, and eye liner and shadow gave her a ghoulish appearance.

*Does this woman own a mirror?*

"Someone should put a sign on that thing," the man old enough to be her father said.

Mildred's daughter, Gail came into the kitchen and pointed at the cooler. "Dad, will you stop fooling around, and put that over in the corner out of the way before someone trips over it?"

A softer version of her mother, except with her father's reddish-blond hair, Gail was a soft spoken, but assured woman who earned, instead of demanded, the respect of those around her.

"Be careful of your back, sweetie." The blonde waved a hand tipped with long fingernails that matched her sweater. "You know how sensitive your back is."

Her hands on her hips, Gail rolled her eyes in Jan and Cameron's direction. Her disgust made it difficult to believe Ralph was her own father.

The blonde giggled while asking him, "I am getting paid for working today, aren't I, Ralphie?"

Gail whirled around on her heels to hear his answer.

"Why, of course, Peggy," Ralph answered. "I wouldn't call you in to work without paying you."

Sparks shot out of Gail's eyes. "This is a charitable operation. *No one* is getting paid. We're doing it to help get the house ready for sale."

Looking Gail up and down, Peggy's lips curled with arrogance. "I don't remember volunteering for anything."

"You didn't have to come if you didn't want to," Gail said. "If you want to spend your day off in bed, then go ahead. I'm sure Dad will be more than happy to keep you company."

"Actually, my darling daughter, we have a lot of work to do down at the office. So we're not going to be able to help today." Ralph looked at the group gathered in the kitchen. "You seem to have enough workers here already. Come along, Peggy. Let's get to work on those claims."

"See you." Like a devoted puppy, the blonde followed Ralph out the side door. "Are you sure that's not a skunk?" she asked Donny who was coming in on their way out.

"Why don't you scare him and see what happens?" he called back to them.

Peggy's laughter was heard all the way from the driveway into the kitchen.

Gail squinted at their departure.

"Hey, Ms. Hildebrand, where's your mom?" Donny asked.

Pain seeped into her tone, when she replied, "I hope she's not around to see them."

Through the door, Donny watched Ralph and Peggy driving off. "I'm sorry. Tad wants to know what she wants to do with some old lawn furniture out in the garage."

"I'll go find her to ask." Gail hurried off up the stairs.

"What are you doing up on that ladder?" Donny asked Jan. "If Tad saw you up there he'd have a cow."

"Hey, you're not getting a fight from me." Jan stepped down, and Donny grabbed the ladder to climb up to take over emptying the cupboards.

"Anybody hungry?" The cheerful call broke the over-worked mood in the kitchen.

The new arrival to volunteer her services wore her ebony hair in a single braid that fell past her shoulders. The top of her head was adorned in a knitted purple cap that matched the scarf she wore loosely around her neck to hang down to her slender waist. The purple in her cap and scarf matched the stripes in her sweater, which accentuated her plump breasts.

Brianne Davenport flashed everyone a toothy grin.

Time had been kind to Brianne Davenport. It took a second look to see the subtle crows-feet and laugh lines that had crept in over the years to adorn her eyes and mouth. Even in her early fifties, she still had a figure that made young men's mouth's drop and salivate.

Donny stopped in mid-step on the ladder to gaze at the vision.

"I've booked a caterer for the whole day." Seeing the handsome young man, Brianne's voice dropped to a sultry tone. "His truck is in the driveway. He's got food for everyone. Don't worry about paying for it. It's my treat."

"Hey! He's got chili!" someone called from the other room. A stampede of hungry volunteers rushed outside.

"Skunk!" some of the volunteers were heard to scream.

"Cat!" came the reply from those in the know.

"We've only been working for four hours!" Mildred was heard to call after them.

Tad stuck his head in the door. "They have hot chili and sandwiches for anyone who wants them."

Jan followed her husband out the door. "Thanks, Brianne. I really am hungry. Come on, Cameron. Let's get some lunch. It'll feel really good to sit down." She rubbed her pregnant stomach. "I think even the baby's tired."

"Come along, Donny." Cameron touched his arm to break the stare.

"I'll be right there."

Disliking the look in the woman's eye, Cameron didn't move. "You look hungry." She was more displeased by his lack of response while looking the older woman up and down. "I'm Detective Cameron Gates." She wished she had a police shield to flash. "Pennsylvania State Police. I'm afraid I didn't catch your name."

"Brianne Davenport." She took the detective's hand. "I own the winery across the road. Albert and my father used to go fishing together." She cast another smile at the tall young man whose path Cameron was blocking. "Is this your son?"

"Friend," she replied.

"Donny Thornton." He shot his arm over her shoulder to offer Brianne his hand.

"He's sixteen," Cameron announced in a sharp tone.

"My," Brianne gushed. "You're awfully big for your age."

Cameron could feel the heat from his blush against her neck.

Brushing a lock of hair out of her eyes, Brianne stepped in closer. "Do you have your driver's license, Donny?" Upon learning that he did, she said, "I collect antique sports cars. I have seven in my garage across the road, including a Ferrari. I've been told that it's the only one in the area. Would you like to see it? I may even let you take it for a spin."

While Donny chuckled behind her, Cameron stepped in closer to tell her in a low voice, "I have a forty-five caliber Colt semi-automatic in my car. Would you like to see that? I may even let you ride in the back of my police cruiser on the way to the station after arresting you for attempted statutory rape—unless you walk away now."

The two women's eyes locked.

The predatory grin dropped from Brianne's face. "Touchy." She stepped back. Flashing a seductive grin at Donny, she tossed her pig tail over the back of her shoulder. "If you ever want to go for a spin, Donny Thornton, come on by. I'd be glad to let you go for a ride."

"That would be great." He stepped forward to follow her out only to find Cameron's arm blocking him like a gate. "What's wrong with you?"

"You stay away from her." With each word, she made her point by jabbing him in his muscular chest with her index finger.

"Why?"

"She's bad news."

"You don't even know her or anything about her," he replied. "What makes you think she's bad news?"

"I can tell."

"I think you're jealous because she's rich and gorgeous."

"More like I'm suspicious because she's hitting on a teenager young enough to be her son."

Donny's eyes grew wide. "Really? She was hitting on me? Do you really think—"

"Whoa, cowboy!" Cameron grabbed the front of his shirt and yanked to force him to bend over so that she could tell him face-to-face. "You better lasso in those hormones right now. If I catch you anywhere near that cougar—"

"Josh!" Doris came up the stairs from the cellar. Her eyes grew wide when she saw them. Cameron still had the young man's sweatshirt balled up in her fist. "Where's Josh?"

"Probably outside eating." Cameron released Donny. "Is there anything I can do for you, Ms. Sullivan?"

"I wanted his opinion about something that I found downstairs." Doris turned to lead her down the stairs.

When Donny attempted to go outside, Cameron, fearful that Brianne would corner him, grabbed his wrist to drag him along with her. They made their way down the dark brick stairwell that creaked with each step they took. She could feel the rotted planks giving way under her weight.

"Geez," Donny gasped when he saw the assortment of belongings in the cellar. "I guess this is what happens when you don't clean your room."

The piles of stuff were up to the ceiling. Halloween decorations. Christmas trees. Board games. Puzzles. There was also a wide assortment of dismantled small appliances. It appeared as if Albert Gordon tried to fix things when they broke instead of buying new.

"It's pretty bad." Doris went to a pile of clothes in the next room and turned on the overhead light. "What do you think I should do with these clothes? Should I stuff them in the garbage bags or take them to Goodwill?"

Cameron's answer was a gasp.

As the light bulb illuminated the room, it lit up the item that wasn't stacked on top of the piles of clothes, but instead, secured to the ceiling beam beside it. It was several sticks of dynamite sealed together with duct tape and wired to an alarm clock. The beating of Cameron's heart drowned out the ticking from the clock.

"Bomb!" Donny yelled.

"What?" Doris looked around.

Cameron pointed with one hand while grabbing Donny with the other. "It's a bomb! We have to get out of here!"

"Oh, no!" Grabbing her bag, Doris ran back into the other room and up the stairs.

Donny pushed Cameron ahead of him to ascend the stairs. In their haste, the rotting steps gave way under Cameron's feet and collapsed to send her falling into his arms. Both of them fell to the floor.

Without looking back, Doris Sullivan disappeared up the stairs. They could hear her steps running on the floor above them.

"She left us!" Donny gasped. "She's gone! She left us down here!" Stunned by her abandonment, he stared up the useless stairs. "I don't believe—"

"*I'm* not leaving you." Cameron grabbed his hand. "There's got to be another way out."

Upstairs, tears streaming down her face, Doris screamed while she ran from one room to the other on the ground floor. "There's a bomb downstairs! We have to get out of the house! There's a bomb in the basement!"

Tad caught Doris in his arms when she raced into the foyer. "A what?"

"A bomb! Downstairs! That police detective found it. She's still down there with Donny!"

"Did you see it?"

"We all saw it!" The elderly woman's body trembled. "The stairs broke, and they're still down there with it!"

In a booming voice, Tad yelled up the stairs that everyone was to leave the house. "Everybody out! Now! There's a bomb downstairs! Grab your butts and get out—go down to the road at the end of the driveway. Now!"

While the volunteers stampeded out, Tad searched for Joshua to tell him that his son and girlfriend were trapped downstairs with the bomb.

Out in the road at the end of the driveway, Joshua was looking to identify who was missing while ushering everyone back from the house when Jan rushed up to him. She was holding her cell phone to her ear. "Josh, Donny and Cameron are downstairs in the basement with the bomb. The stairs collapsed and they can't get out. They're trapped."

His heart racing, Joshua fled up the driveway.

He and Tad ran around to the back door that went down a set of cement steps into the cellar. The sound of a window shattering came to their ears when they rounded the corner. The door had been padlocked shut from the outside, but Donny had found a sledge hammer to break the window pane.

After helping Cameron crawl out through the window pane and jump down, Joshua and Tad helped Donny squeeze his broad shoulders through the opening. "How much time do we have?" Tad asked Cameron.

"I don't know. I didn't take the time to check out the timer."

The four of them made a wide berth of the house while running around to the front and down the driveway to the road where the volunteers were waiting.

After everyone hugged and assured each other that they were safe, a silence fell over the group of volunteers. Cameron clutched Irving in her arms. Then, after the adrenalin wore off, they waited for the police to arrive or the house to blow up or for something to happen to justify the panic they had suffered. A murmur traveled through the crowd and eyes turned to Cameron, who had initiated the exodus from the house.

Even Irving eyed his mistress from where he had climbed up onto Donny's shoulders to drape his body around his neck. His tail twitched from where it hung down to below Donny's chest.

The murmur grew to a question that Tad was brave enough to voice. "Cam, are you sure that was a bomb you saw?"

"Yes, I'm sure it was a bomb," she replied with her hands on her hips.

The glare in Joshua's eyes matched those of Irving's when he asked, "Do you even know what a bomb looks like?"

The house exploded into a fireball. The roof went straight up into the air. The windows shot straight out in every direction.

As if the bomb was under him, Irving sprang from where he had been lounging around Donny's shoulders and landed in Cameron's arms.

The blast hit the catering truck to detonate the gas tank and kerosene to set it ablaze, which rapidly spread to the garage.

"What a bummer," Brianne Davenport said to the caterer, whose eyes popped open wide and mouth dropped open at the sight.

Out in the road, Joshua shoved Cameron and Donny down to the ground and threw himself spread eagle over both of them. The heat from the blast washed over them like a tidal wave.

The deafening explosion shook Snowden Road to be followed by silence that seemed to encompass the whole countryside.

Within moments, Albert's home, garage, and the catering truck were engulfed in a total inferno.

Turning to Joshua, Cameron broke the silence. "Does that answer your question?"

# Chapter Three

**One Week Later**

Pennsylvania State Police's crime lab was still sorting through the debris of what had once been Albert Gordon's farmhouse for evidence of who and why someone had blown up the elderly man's home after his death. An already difficult job was made more challenging by the volume of junk that had been catapulted across the countryside by the bomb's blast.

Detective Cameron Gates took the lead for the investigation since she was on the scene at the time of the explosion. Based on Albert Gordon's long career as a criminal lawyer, she concentrated on looking through his background for disgruntled clients who may have sought revenge for a case lost. After a week, she was still empty-handed on leads or suspects.

After a long day of reading one ancient case file after another, Cameron went to Joshua's home, a three-story stone house located on the corner of Rock Spring Boulevard and Fifth Street in Chester.

Friday night had become their date-in night. Unless he was in court, Joshua would work remotely at home and cook dinner for him, Cameron, Donny, Admiral, and Irving, who would spend the evening glaring at *the other man* who had come into his life. After dinner, the cat would curl up on the chair in Joshua's study and sulk.

The scent of roasted chicken embraced Cameron like a mother's loving arms when Donny greeted her at the front door. Her stomach growled to remind her that all she had eaten that day was a bag of tortilla chips with hot and spicy salsa.

On his way up the stairs to his room, Donny gestured down the hallway toward the kitchen. "Dad's about done cooking dinner."

In the Thornton kitchen, she found Joshua standing over a pot of homemade giblet gravy. The Thornton's Irish Wolfhound-Great Dane mix, Admiral, was sitting next to him with his eyes focused on the pot. Irving had jumped up onto a window sill. His tail twitching, he eyed the gravy.

Joshua was tearing off bites of the warm French bread and dipping them into the pan of gravy before eating them. It was a habit left over from his childhood. As a boy, he had to taste his grandmother's cooking before it was served to make sure it was cooked right. "You caught me." He popped a second bite of gravy soaked bread into his mouth. "I can't resist." He dipped a bite of the bread in the gravy and tossed it in Admiral's direction. The dog caught it in mid-air.

When Irving stretched out a paw as far as he could without falling off the window sill, Joshua tossed a bite doused in gravy, which the cat caught in his mouth, and then dropped. His whiskers soaked with gravy, he jumped to the floor to retrieve the morsel. He then tried to pick it up with his paws, only to get them wet. The cat shot Joshua a glare as if to say, "Why didn't you tell me this was so messy?" He bit into the bread, shook it, and then proceeded to work on eating it bite by bite.

Meanwhile, Admiral was stomping his big feet to demand his next serving.

Ignoring the two of them, Joshua cut off a slice of the bread, dipped it in the gravy, and fed it to Cameron. She had barely swallowed before he kissed the gravy from her lips.

"Yummy." She sliced off a helping of the bread that was still warm to the touch. "They've finished tearing down the house, and the state police are now going through Albert's basement. They found parts of a square alarm clock. I recognized it as the timer on the bomb. With so much garbage in that basement, forensics has a lot to sort through to find the explosives, but they'll get it done."

"It doesn't make sense," he said. "Albert led a completely low-risk lifestyle. He was as clean as a whistle. His closest friends were his neighbors who lived up and down Snowden Road, and they've all known each other their whole adult lives. That's an old road out in the boonies."

"Most everyone who lives around there is born and dies there," Cameron said.

"Albert has been dead for almost a month," he said. "If one of his clients wanted revenge, why blow up his house after he's already dead? It isn't like it's hurting *him* any. I have yet to find one person who has ever been inside. Which leaves another question? When was that bomb planted?"

"And why was it set to detonate when the house was filled with people? I'm beginning to think one of us was the intended victim." She tore off a bite of bread and tossed it at Admiral, who seemed to swallow it without chewing.

Now finished with his helping, Irving jumped up and stretched the length of his body until his front paws were almost to the edge of the counter. Cameron tore off a crust, dabbed it with the gravy, and handed it to the cat.

"Only someone who was totally evil would have killed a dozen innocent people in order to get one," Joshua said.

"I've come up against perps like that."

"And I've prosecuted a few," he said. "Could whoever blew up his house have also killed Albert? The bomb could have been to get rid evidence revealing his crime? Maybe your ME missed something."

"Already thought of that." Cameron cut a second slice of bread to split between them. "After the explosion I asked her to take a second look at Gordon. Findings were the same. He had a stroke and had fallen down the front stairs, which caused the avalanche of newspapers that smothered him. Cause of death: asphyxiation."

Joshua shrugged. "Well, if I can be of any help ..."

"Tell me about Brianne Davenport." The corner of her lips curled when she saw his hand, clutching a juicy bite of bread dipped in gravy, freeze in mid-air. "Donny did tell you about that pass she made at him?"

Admiral inched forward with expectation in his eyes.

"He's rather proud of it." Joshua double dunked the piece of bread. "Whoever would have thought? A real live cougar right here in Chester." He tossed the bread into his mouth.

Admiral groaned.

"Actually, she lives in Hookstown," Cameron noted, "my jurisdiction."

"She's old enough to be Donny's mother."

"I'm glad you noticed that," she said. "Your son doesn't strike me as the type to date a cougar."

"I don't want him dating a cougar," he agreed, "especially *that* cougar. For one, she's married."

"To whom?"

"Ned Carter. He's the manager at the Mountaineer Casino. Real slick guy. I don't trust him."

"They sound like a nice couple," she said with sarcasm. "Maybe you should lock Donny up until this case is closed."

"As flattered as Donny is by the attention of an older gorgeous woman, he's still got the cool Thornton head on his shoulders." He wrapped his arms around her. "Don't worry. You'd be surprised how fast Donny can run. She's not going to catch him, especially in those high heels she wears."

She looked into his blue eyes. "You still haven't told me about her. What scares you about this particular cougar besides her being married?"

"Brianne Davenport owns Davenport Winery." With one arm wrapped around her waist, he tore off a bite of the bread with one hand and tossed it into her mouth.

Again, Admiral groaned.

Irving was less pitiful and more demanding. There was a rumble deep in his chest that grew into a loud howl followed by a hiss.

Releasing her, Joshua told Irving, "She's mine. Get over it."

"Davenport Winery," she said, "which is across the street from Albert's modest farm on Snowden Road. Davenport wines are sold all over."

"World-wide distribution," he said. "They have several farms all over Pennsylvania to grow different types of grapes. They're listed on most restaurants' wine lists. Brianne inherited all of it when her daddy died of a heart attack several years ago. She was only twenty-two years old and took her family's little winery world-wide. Business exploded when the Internet came about. They went public a dozen years ago. She is a very savvy business woman."

"She's rich, savvy, and likes handsome, young men," she said. "What else?"

"The Mountaineer is being investigated by the state prosecutor's office for embezzlement. My office isn't involved, but the state attorney general told them to keep me informed about it."

"Who initiated the investigation?"

"That, I don't know," Joshua said. "It's been in the news. Some leaks to the media have said that the forensics auditors are finding evidence of money being skimmed from accounts going back more than a decade."

"Sounds like Ned Carter's got his hands full," Cameron said. "Maybe that's why his wife is chasing after teenaged boys. Since the Mountaineer is on your side of the state line, do you mind if I poke around and ask a few questions about Ned Carter and his wife?"

He grinned. "You want to keep an eye on Brianne to keep her away from Donny."

"Do you mind?"

He kissed her on the cheek. "Does that answer your question?"

Without knocking to announce his arrival, Tad threw open the back door, saw, and smelled the pot on the stove. "Is that chicken gravy and fresh French bread?"

As part of his domestication that came with marriage, Tad had bought the red brick house next door to Joshua's stone home on Rock Spring Boulevard. The location made for a convenient jog across his driveway to grab a meal when Jan was working late as news editor at *The Review*, the newspaper that served the tri-state area. Its offices were across the river in East Liverpool, Ohio.

Cameron broke off a helping of bread and offered it to Tad. The doctor fell into line with her squeezed between the two men.

Joshua yelled up the stairs. "Donny, dinner's ready." The sound of running feet told them that the growing teenager had been waiting for the call.

Admiral took his spot next to what had become Cameron's chair at the kitchen table. She was a pushover for hand-outs. Likewise, Irving took his spot on the other side of her chair.

While Joshua served the food onto the table, Cameron's cell phone rang. "Rats," she said while putting it to her ear.

"I am so glad Tracy taught you how to cook," Tad told Joshua while admiring the beautiful golden skin on the roast chicken.

"I am, too," Donny said. "I'd have starved to death by now if she hadn't."

Tad took a seat at what had become his place at the Thornton table.

After observing the food that was only moments from making its way to her plate, Cameron announced that she had to leave. "What's the last thing you'd want to find under the rumble of an exploded house?"

"A dead body," Tad chuckled.

"But that isn't possible," Donny said. "No one was in Albert's house when it blew up. At least, no one has been reported missing."

Without humor, Cameron nodded her head. "Well, that's exactly what they found in your cousin Albert's basement—a dead body."

# Chapter Four

"Unbelievable." Joshua stepped back from the open freezer to let the Pennsylvania State Police medical examiner get to work.

Tad peered over the medical examiner's shoulder to get a closer look at the body. Since Hookstown was out of his jurisdiction, he wasn't allowed to touch. He could only watch another medical examiner work what was her crime scene.

It was killing him. This wasn't his case. However, Albert Gordon was family. Professionally and personally, he wanted to dive in to clear his cousin's name.

Out of professional courtesy, Cameron had permitted them to ride along to the scene. In exchange, they would be expected to allow her the same leeway if she needed help in their jurisdiction.

The dented and charred ice box was one of the few things that had survived the explosion intact. The chief forensics officer told Cameron that it had been found tucked away in a room separate from the one in which the bomb had been placed. Even though the upper floors had collapsed on top of it, the drywall and mounds of junk surrounding it had protected the freezer from the explosion and fire.

Upon its discovery, the investigators pulled it out from the corner and opened it. The smell of death burst forth like evil escaping from Pandora's box. After regaining their senses, they peered inside to find a body encased in a stark white tomb.

She looked like she had crawled in and curled up to take a nap. Her makeup was still evident on her leathered flesh. They could see the blue of her eye shadow and thick false eyelashes. Her hair was draped over her face and shoulders. Its platinum color created the illusion of a mermaid captured in a fisherman's icy net.

Her jeans and matching vest were faded and discolored to the point of only holding a hint of their original hue, but intact. To fit into the tight confines of the freezer, she was curled up into the fetal position with her high-heeled sandals still on her feet. Her denim hat rested on her knees.

Cameron was gesturing at the now empty corner of the hole in the ground that had once been Albert's basement. "Was this thing plugged in when the bomb went off?" She couldn't see any sign of an electrical outlet where they had found the appliance.

With a shake of his head, the officer said, "There was no outlet near it. We found the cord wrapped up and tucked in behind the freezer. You can see the thing is ancient. I doubt if it works."

Observing the wrecked condition of the appliance, Cameron said, "Certainly not now."

The photo recordings of the scene completed, the medical examiner started her physical on-scene examination of the body.

Tad watched her. "Any ID on her?"

"Maybe." She reached down along the wall of the freezer and removed a blue canvas purse covered with beads. She handed it to the detective. "Let's hope we get lucky, and she has the name of her killer in there." The medical examiner continued to search the body.

Having no convenient place in the burnt-out basement to spread out the purse's contents, Cameron climbed out of the foundation to empty the purse on the hood of her cruiser. With her gloved fingers, she picked through the assortment of what appeared to be the usual feminine fare, except for a few additional surprises. There was a pack of Camel cigarettes, a bag of marijuana with a couple of hand-rolled cigarettes, a wallet, and various cosmetics.

With gloved hands, Joshua picked up the pack of cigarettes. "We can trace the lot number on this pack of cigarettes to find out when they were made to give us an approximate time period of when she was killed."

"I think you meant me. This isn't your case, Mr. Thornton. So put that back." Cameron was already checking out the driver's license in the wallet.

Joshua placed the cigarettes back in the pile.

"Got a name, Cam?" Tad asked.

"California driver's license. Expiration date: June 1985. Name: Cherry Pickens," she answered.

Tad responded to the announcement with a wicked laugh.

"What's so funny, Doc?" she asked.

Tad regarded the two of them. "We just solved a famous unsolved mystery."

"*Famous* unsolved mystery?" Joshua parroted.

Tad gestured to the freezer. "Take a look, ladies and gentlemen. You are looking at Cherry Pickens, a genuine film legend."

"*Cherry Pickens*," Cameron countered. "Never heard of her."

"You wouldn't unless you were into porn," Tad said.

"I didn't know you were into porn," Joshua said with a frown.

"I'm not into porn," Tad replied, "but I am into rock and roll. Back in the early eighties, Cherry Pickens was one of the brightest stars of artistic films." He held up his fingers in the form of quotation marks when he used the word "artistic".

"Sex, drugs, and rock and roll," Joshua said.

Tad nodded his head in agreement. "Drugs are a big part of the scene in pornography, and Cherry Pickens was in it up to her pretty blue eyeballs." He added, "But she wasn't just a hooker who did it on film. They have film awards, and she won a couple. In some circles, she was considered a true actress with the talent to break through into legitimate movies."

Cameron brought them back to the present. "How did she end up in a freezer, in a farmhouse, in Hookstown, Pennsylvania?"

"That's for you to find out," Tad told her.

"You said she'd won acting awards," Cameron reminded him. "Are you saying she was actually famous?"

"She slept with all the big hard core rock musicians, most of whom are now has-beens, the ones who didn't OD or kill themselves that is," Tad said. "Humphrey Phoenix, the owner of *Player* magazine, discovered her when she was dancing at one of his sex parties—"

"Now I heard of him," Cameron said.

"*Player* magazine was about as hard core porn as you can get," Tad said. "Humphrey Phoenix was twenty years older than Cherry. He spent a lot of money on her. Then he found out that she was also fooling around with a pop singer while Phoenix was paying for her breast implants and nose job. The FBI believed Phoenix made an example of her by making her disappear."

"Hookstown is a long way from Hollywood," Joshua said. "What would a missing porn star be doing here in Cousin Albert's basement?"

They stared at Tad who had no answer.

"If what you're saying is true," Cameron said, "this could be a mob hit, which would make this the fed's turf." She sucked in her breath. She really didn't want the FBI butting their way into one of her cases.

"Albert had no ties to any of that," Tad told them. "Until the forensics pathologist gets a go at her, we can't determine the time of death. She could have played it smart and managed to get away from the mob only to get killed over something else years afterwards."

"I don't believe this," Joshua muttered.

Stretching her back, which had become sore from bending over into the freezer, the medical examiner said, "Right now, the way she's positioned in this freezer, I can't find the cause of death. I need to do a full examination at the state lab."

Joshua went over to peer into the freezer. "Can you find any evidence of sexual assault?"

The examiner poked at the clothes on the body. "Her clothes don't seem to be disturbed."

Joshua studied the cap, which contained silk lining. "Looks expensive."

"They are." With the point of her pen, the medical examiner opened the jean vest. "These jeans have a designer label. This lady had the best in clothes."

"But what was she doing dying here?" Joshua asked.

"And in your cousin's basement?" Cameron asked. "And was she the reason his house was blown sky high?"

"I think it's safe to assume she was," Joshua said. "As big as that blast was, whoever it was clearly wanted everything destroyed."

"How ironic that the only thing not destroyed was this freezer," the detective said.

"I can't imagine Albert not noticing that freezer in his basement," said Tad.

"Come on," she countered. "You saw his basement. The only reason this freezer survived was because it was surrounded by a whole bunch of stuff that cushioned the impact. Maybe it was behind all that stuff in order to hide it from Albert. How long had he been living here?"

"As long as I can remember," Joshua answered. "I can see it in the headlines now."

In a gentle tone, Cameron told them, "At some point, we will have to release the name of the victim. When we do that, your cousin will be declared a closet sex fiend. Suggestions will be made that we dig up the floor with speculation that there are a dozen other women buried under the concrete."

"Albert was no sex fiend," Tad said.

Joshua agreed with his cousin. "We've known Albert all our lives. He didn't even date after his wife died."

"Publicly," Cameron said. "That's what they thought about John Wayne Gacy, and he butchered over thirty-three boys in his house, and the neighbors had no idea."

"Albert was no killer," Tad said. "He went to our church."

"The BTK killer was an elder in his church," Cameron said in a steady tone.

Unable to find words to argue in the face of her facts, Tad sighed. "Josh, you knew Albert. Tell her. He wasn't a killer."

"No, he wasn't." Joshua placed his hands on her shoulders. "Help us."

"How?" She held her breath.

"Keep this under wraps as long as you can."

"That goes without saying."

In a soft voice, he said, "Give us as much time and information as you can, to find out who did this."

"*You* find out who did this?" she replied. "You keep forgetting that this is *my* case. You two shouldn't even be here."

Joshua corrected himself. "Then *you* find out who did this. But, in the meantime, you keep this under wraps."

"Are you talking cover-up?" She shook her head. "I can't go—"

"Professional courtesy?" Joshua said. "We'll pay you back when your cases come over to our side."

She glanced over at Tad. "When I need info from forensics in West-by-God-Virginia ..."

"It's yours." He nodded his head.

Joshua cocked his head at her. "What do you say?"

The corner of her lip curled as it always did when a wicked thought crossed her mind. "Come over to my place later, and we'll talk about it," she said in a low, sultry voice.

# Chapter Five

They were two of a kind. Early in their relationship, Joshua was delighted to discover that Cameron's love for ice cream and other good foods matched his.

For this date, they were sharing a sundae-for-two at Cricksters, a retro ice cream and sandwich diner on the West Virginia side of the state line along Route 30. Cricksters was *their* place.

The sundae they were sharing was a special order that they had created, which the servers had come to call "The C & J Lovers' Delight". The dessert consisted of three scoops of Hershey's Vanilla Ice Cream in a waffle bowl, served with banana, hot fudge sauce, whipped cream, nuts, miniature chocolate chips, and two cherries on top.

The lady in the freezer had been sent to the state lab to be examined by a forensic pathologist. As soon as she got the medical examiner's report, Cameron had called Joshua to drive up from his office in New Cumberland to meet her. She'd brought along a copy of the report in a manila envelope for him to read between spoonfuls of ice cream.

On his way in from the parking lot, Joshua tried to ignore Irving's glare from the front seat of her cruiser. The cat's feeling of being betrayed by his mistress, who had left him in the car to cool his paws in the cold winter weather while meeting *the other man,* was so intense that Joshua could sense it.

At the door, Joshua paused and looked over his shoulder to see if the pair of emerald eyeballs he felt boring a hole in his back was imagined. It wasn't. Irving was sitting on top of the back seat, his eyes directed straight at him. His long tail twitched. "That is one creepy cat," he muttered before going inside.

She was waiting at what had unofficially become their booth. After greeting her with a kiss, Joshua saw that the server was already building their sundae behind the counter. After taking off his coat, which he folded and tucked into the corner of the booth, he slid into the seat on the other side of the table.

"First off," Cameron began, "the drivers' license was a fake."

"Then she wasn't the porn star," Joshua said, after their server delivered the sundae.

"Wrong there. Our victim *was* Cherry Pickens." She opened the envelope. "Her disappearance was big news back then. Since she was a celebrity, it wasn't hard for me to dig up her past in a background check. Most of my work had already been done when she went missing. While it wasn't complete, it was thorough enough to give me a good start. Cherry Pickens was her screen name."

"Why didn't we already know that?" he asked. "Cherry Pickens. Perfect name for a sex film star."

"Cherry Pickens first appeared on the scene in 1980," she recounted from her report. "She starred in Humphrey Phoenix's first X-rated production. *Sugar Sugar.* Up until then, he was only into porn magazines. With Cherry Pickens as his star, he became a movie producer."

"Where did he find her?" Joshua asked. "Tad said she'd been discovered at a party."

Cameron slid the police report across to his side of the table. "According to her press releases, she was the daughter of a Texas oil man. She ran off to Hollywood to work as an actress and model. A friend had invited her to one of Phoenix's parties, which was where he discovered her on the dance floor. She became rich and famous overnight until she ticked her sugar daddy off, and he decided to have her killed."

Joshua studied another portion of the autopsy report. "How long had she been dead?"

Despite the written report in front of him, Cameron said, "That's hard to say. Contrary to what we first thought, the body was never frozen; but that freezer was air-tight. No bugs or critters to tamper with the body … or the evidence. If she hadn't been put in that air-tight freezer, all of that evidence would have been destroyed over time, including her fingerprints. Whoever put her in there literally put her in a time capsule. Lucky thing for us."

"Being air-tight, that meant nothing could get out," Joshua said. "That's why the smell was so rancid when the freezer was opened."

"Oh, yeah," she replied. "I've narrowed the estimated time of death down to the summer of 1985."

"You did? Why the summer of '85? Because that's when she went missing?"

"That, plus the tobacco manufacturer says the cigarettes we found in her purse were made in the spring of that year. Nothing in her purse was made later than May 1985. Combine that with it being the last time she was seen alive …" She lifted her shoulders. "I think it's a good assumption … even though *you* never assume"

Joshua was impressed. "Cause of death?"

She paused to spoon a mouthful of ice cream with hot fudge dripping from it into her mouth. "Cherry was a real party girl. There was enough heroin in her system that she would have OD'd. They found tracks in between her toes and under her armpits. Her lungs showed that she had been a heavy smoker. Her nasal passages were like Swiss cheese from cocaine. Her blood alcohol level was .27. But none of that was what killed her. Her neck was snapped and her spinal cord broken. ME said it wasn't a twist. It was like a sharp blow to the back of the neck with something hard, heavy, and sharp—like a spade or shovel. Death would have been instantaneous."

Joshua reached across the table to wipe a drip of hot fudge from her chin and lick it off the tip of his finger. "With all that alcohol and drugs in her system, maybe she fell and struck the back of her neck against something like the edge of a table. A defense attorney could argue that it was an accident."

"Yeah, right," she replied.

He cocked his head and an eyebrow at her.

"Now, for the answer to the $20 million dollar question." She flashed him a grin. "What was a porn star doing in a freezer, in your cousin's basement in Hookstown?"

Grinning, he sat back and folded his arms across his chest. "What was a porn star doing in a freezer, in my cousin's basement in Hookstown?"

"While her publicist told one story, her fingerprints tell another." She scooped up another helping of ice cream.

"They were able to lift her fingerprints," Joshua said.

Her mouth full with ice cream and hot fudge, Cameron nodded her head.

While waiting for her to swallow, he turned around the report to read the answer for himself. "AFIS got a match."

She dug to the bottom of the bowl for the hot fudge that had slid off the ice cream. "Back in late 1979, Cheryl Smith was arrested in Los Angeles for prostitution and possession of cocaine. The charges were dropped. Six months later, *Sugar Sugar* was released by Humphrey Phoenix with Cherry Pickens as the star. Phoenix had a lot of people on his payroll, including crooked cops and politicians. I know it's only circumstantial, but I would conclude that Cheryl Smith was a high class call girl who found herself a big sugar daddy, who reinvented her, complete with a new identity."

Joshua put down his spoon. "Cheryl Smith?"

Cameron flipped the pages of the report. "When you get arrested, not only do you supply your fingerprints, but you also give your social security number. With that, I was able to do a background check. I think I know what Cheryl Smith was doing here when she was killed."

"This is her hometown."

She looked up from the report to him. Her left eyebrow arched. "You know that already."

"Cheryl Smith was from this area," he said.

She closed the folder and slid the ice cream over to her side of the table. "Now it's your turn to report what you know." The spoon was full of hot fudge sauce that she brought to her mouth.

"I was in middle school when Angie Sullivan disappeared," he said.

Cameron paused with the spoon in her mouth. She saw sadness in his eyes. She lowered the spoon. "Did you know Angie?"

"Barely." He shook his head. "Tad knew her, though. He was at Melody Lane Skating Rink when she had that fight with Cheryl Smith."

"After which Angie Sullivan disappeared."

"I was in high school when her body turned up," he said. "We had a drought the summer before my senior year. The Ohio River got the lowest that it had ever been. That was when they found her car—and her body—off the bank along the yacht club. Of course, by then, Cheryl Smith was nowhere to be found."

"Because she was in Hollywood making movies under a new identity."

"Doris Sullivan is Angie's sister," he said.

Cameron nodded her head. "The same Doris Sullivan who happened to be on the scene of the explosion meant to destroy Cheryl Smith's body."

"If Cheryl killed Angie, then Doris had a strong motive for killing her."

She asked, "Was there any connection between Cheryl Smith and Albert Gordon?"

Joshua answered by taking out his cell phone. "I was only a kid when all that happened with Cheryl Smith. Tad would remember better than I would." After hitting the speaker button, he placed the phone in the middle of the table.

After a few pleasantries, Cameron reported the real name of the victim in the freezer. There was a long silence from the other end of the line before Tad responded, "Really? Cheryl Smith, huh?"

"Cheryl Smith," Joshua said.

"Cherry Pickens was Cheryl Smith?" the doctor asked. "Who would have thought? Are you sure? I knew Cheryl Smith."

Cameron explained, "One, she was mummified when you saw her in the freezer. Two, she'd had a whole lot of cosmetic surgery. The ME says she had a nose job and chin job, not to mention the always reliable breast implants. So if you saw any of her movies—"

"I *never* saw any of her movies," Tad replied firmly.

Joshua smiled at the defensive tone in his cousin's voice.

The detective asked, "Here's what I need to know. What connection was there between Cheryl Smith and your cousin Albert Gordon?"

A deep naughty laugh came out of the phone. "Not the type of connection you're looking for. Albert was a straight-up guy. But he was her lawyer."

Joshua gasped. "Her lawyer? But she was never arrested for Angie's murder. She was long gone when Angie's body was found."

"I'm talking about before that—back when Angie first disappeared," Tad explained. "The summer that Angie disappeared—I think it was 1978—Cheryl was at the top of the suspect list."

"But she had an alibi," Cameron said.

"Right," Tad said. "But her alibi was her derelict friends, so no one bought it. Anyway, there wasn't enough to arrest her. Angie was gone so there was no evidence. There were no witnesses. Suddenly, days after Angie's gone missing, Cheryl's making plans to move to Hollywood and leave the area. The prosecutor in Beaver County didn't want her going anywhere, so he tried to get an injunction to make her stay. That was where Albert came in. He defended Cheryl at the hearing, and the judge said with no real evidence to connect Cheryl to Angie's disappearance; they couldn't prevent her from leaving the area. Days later, Cheryl's gone, and just like the prosecutor predicted, she disappeared off the grid."

Joshua concluded, "When Angie's body turned up in 1984, Cheryl Smith was nowhere to be found."

Tad asked, "Why would she come back here ... of all places?"

Cameron said, "If we find the answer to that, then we'll find the answer to how she ended up in that cellar."

"Albert had nothing more to do with Cheryl after she left town," Tad said. "He lost more than one friend for defending her at that hearing."

Cameron bit her tongue to keep from voicing that as a possible motive for Albert killing Cheryl Smith. The passion in Tad's tone warned of an argument that she didn't want to fight with Joshua on the scene.

Announcing that he had a patient waiting for him, Tad disconnected their conversation.

Joshua tapped the button to turn off the phone with the handle of his spoon before finishing off the last of the sundae. "Any other leads?"

"I found this when I went through her clothes." She handed him a sheet of paper. "I made a copy for you."

Joshua studied the image of both sides of a business card.

"I found it in the back pocket of Cheryl's jeans," she explained. "The lab was able to augment it enough to read the writing on the back."

The printing on the front of the card was simple. It read: *Davenport Winery*. On the next line it read: *Brianne Davenport, Owner*. *Direct Line* was written in the corner along with the phone number.

"Brianne Davenport was good friends with Angie." Joshua read the cursive writing on the back of the card. It read *Ned* and had another phone number.

"I checked out the phone number," she told him. "It's disconnected now, but back in the summer of 1985, it belonged to Ned Carter's car phone."

"Brianne's husband." He set down his spoon to concentrate on the report. "I remember he used to deal drugs back in the day—very small time—mainly to his friends, which is why he was so popular."

"Cheryl had to have gotten that heroin from someone," Cameron said. "She didn't crawl into that freezer in Albert's cellar on her own. Somebody hid her body there—Maybe to make a statement about him defending her."

Joshua studied the picture of the lady. "She used to be very pretty. Too bad she screwed it up."

"Yes, she was very pretty," she said. "Best looks money can buy."

Cameron turned her attention to the waffle dish. She broke it apart with her spoon to eat. Joshua wasn't a fan of the waffle dish. The rest was hers and hers alone.

Joshua was still studying the pictures. "Any indications of sexual assault?"

"No tears in her clothes or wounding in the pelvic area," she said. "There was some seminal fluid. So she did have sex shortly before her death. They got enough to get his DNA." She shook her spoon at him. "Lucky thing for us."

"Us?" he asked.

"Angie Sullivan's body was found at the yacht club," she said. "That's Chester, West Virginia. Your turf. That makes her murder your case. Don't you want to tag along with me, just in case I uncover something that could solve her murder?" She batted her eye lashes at him. "I promise you'll have a good time."

Smirking at her, Joshua slid the report to the side and reached across the table for her hand. "If the killer placed that freezer in Albert's basement to make a point, then why did they try to destroy it by blowing up half the countryside?"

"That's something we're going to have to find out." She picked up the report and put it back into the envelope. "Do you want to go on a road trip with me?"

"To where?"

"Down memory lane."

"Is Irving going with us?" Joshua asked.

Seeing the look in his eye, she hesitated before replying, "Are you willing to accept the pay back if we leave him behind at your place?"

Joshua sat up straight. "I'm a man. I can take it."

"That's what you always say."

❧ ❧ ❧ ❧

Cameron found retired Pennsylvania State Police Detective Harry Shannon tinkering under a 1972 Charger. His wife had directed Cameron and Joshua around to the garage located behind their white ranch-style home in the suburbs of Raccoon Township, Pennsylvania. Inside the garage, they found a dismantled red and white muscle car with a man's legs sticking out from underneath it.

"Detective Shannon?" Cameron bent over to call underneath the car while Joshua admired its leather interior.

"Not anymore, lady."

She held out her badge under the car for the man to see. "I'm Detective Cameron Gates from the Pennsylvania State Police. Homicide. I left a message with your wife earlier about Angelina Sullivan's murder." She gestured at the pair of feet on the other side of the car. "This is Joshua Thornton, a prosecutor from Hancock County—"

"This ain't his jurisdiction."

"Her body was found in the Ohio River along the banks of Chester, West Virginia," Joshua called down to him. "It's believed she was killed in Chester, which *makes* it *my* jurisdiction."

The dolly slid out from under the car to reveal a muscular, bald man with a white goatee and mustache. Small wire-rimmed glasses were perched on his nose. "What's this about?"

"We found Cheryl Smith," Cameron said. "Your prime suspect."

"You found Cheryl Smith? Are you sure?"

"We're sure," Cameron said.

"I'll be damned." The retired detective wiped his hands on a rag he had resting on his stomach. He climbed to his feet. He looked from one of them to the other and back again while scratching his head. "Where is she?"

Joshua asked him, "Did you hear about the explosion in Hookstown a couple of weeks ago?"

"No one was hurt in that."

"A dead body was found in a freezer in the basement of that house, which happened to have been the home of Albert Gordon, Smith's lawyer," she said. "The victim was identified as Cheryl Smith—the same Cheryl Smith wanted for questioning in Angelina Sullivan's murder."

Pacing the garage, Harry rubbed his goatee while repeating, "I'll be damned. I'll be damned."

Cameron and Joshua exchanged glances. She stepped into the path of his pacing to rip him from his thoughts. "In order for us to determine if Cheryl Smith's murder was connected to Angie Sullivan's murder, we need to know what you remember from your investigation of her disappearance."

"I'm retired." Harry said.

"You were the first lead investigator in the case," Joshua said. "You were there at the beginning. That makes this case your baby."

"Don't tell me that baby doesn't wake you up at night," she added. "Disappearance of a young girl in her prime. Years later, she's found dumped in the river."

A slow grin crossed his tanned face. "Follow me."

He led them through the house's back door into a country kitchen where his wife was baking cookies from scratch. He offered them both seats at the table, in the middle of which he had a case file tied together with a string.

"Angie Sullivan was only eighteen years old," Harry told them. "She had graduated from South Side High school in

Hookstown a couple of weeks before she disappeared, June 3, 1978."

"1978?" Cameron stared at the picture resting on top of the police reports in the case file he had put out for them to examine. It was Angie Sullivan's senior class picture. With her long silky, strawberry-blond hair and blue eyes, she looked like every mother's ideal for a daughter. Wholesome and sweet.

*Too sweet to die so young.*

"Angie disappeared hours after being in a fight with Cheryl Smith, and Cheryl's last words to her were that she wasn't through with her yet. The prosecutor tried to keep her in the area, but her scumbag lawyer got the judge to say she could go."

"That scumbag was my cousin," Joshua said.

Harry apologized. "But you have to understand where I'm coming from."

"I understand," Joshua said, "but with no direct evidence to prove she had anything to do with Angie's disappearance—"

"She was threatening the victim only hours before she disappeared."

"That's circumstantial," the lawyer argued. "Truth is you had nothing, and you can't indefinitely confine a suspect to a town without any real evidence to prove they had anything to do with it. It's been over forty years since Angie Sullivan disappeared and the case is still open. What was Cheryl Smith supposed to do? Put her whole life on hold until you find enough evidence to either arrest her or clear her? That's unfair persecution without—"

Not wanting to waste their time in a debate about law and order, Cameron interjected, "The fact is that after going off to Hollywood to make it big in porn, your prime suspect came back here and ended up dead in a freezer."

"Porn star?" Harry asked.

Joshua said, "Cheryl Smith ended up going to Hollywood, changing her name, and becoming a star in porn movies."

"Sounds like Cheryl Smith," the retired detective said.

Cameron said, "According to the ME's report, she had breast implants and a nose job. Between that and her name change, she was able to keep off the radar in this investigation."

Harry's wife didn't have to offer twice when she set a plate of warm chocolate chip cookies in the center of the table for them to eat.

"You're right," Harry grumbled to Joshua. "We had nothing. Cheryl had a dozen witnesses saying that they were drinking and partying at the First Street Chester Bridge Overlook until way into the middle of the night. She even had a boy saying that they were having intercourse in the back of his van."

Cameron asked, "First Street? In Chester?"

Joshua spoke around a bite of a cookie. "The police are chasing kids out of there all the time. They've torn apart the monument and destroyed it with graffiti."

She was doubtful. "I imagine all of these witnesses that vouched for Cheryl were boy scouts."

"You know how it is," Harry told her. "Since we couldn't disprove their alibis, and with no evidence that anything had actually happened to Angie, we couldn't keep her. The prosecutor tried, but Gordon fought for them to let her go. Less than two weeks after Angie Sullivan disappeared, Cheryl Smith was gone. The case went cold until the drought in 1984 made the water level in the river drop to show her car off the yacht club pier."

"Which happened to be less than a mile downstream from where Cheryl Smith and her friends were partying," Joshua said.

Harry nodded his head vigorously. "By then, Cheryl Smith was nowhere to be found."

"Did her friends give her up after the body turned up?" Cameron asked.

"That's the benefit of time in cold cases," the retired detective answered. "Loyalties have a way of dissolving over the course of years. After Angie's body was found, several of Cheryl's friends did admit that they were all so high and drunk that most of them passed out during the night." With a frown, he shook his head. "But not the Romeo that she was with. That hard ass refused to give her up."

"What were Cheryl and Angie fighting over?" Joshua asked him.

"Cheryl got it in her head that Angie was fooling around with her ex-boyfriend Ned Carter."

"Ned?" Cameron asked.

"He married her best friend Brianne Davenport about a year after Angie disappeared," Harry said.

"Was Angie having an affair with him?"

"According to him, no," Harry said.

"Don't you find it significant that Ned and Brianne were so quick to get married after their friend's disappearance?" Joshua asked.

"Why?" Harry replied. "The beef was between Cheryl and Angie."

"Over Ned, who married Brianne," Joshua pointed out.

Cameron picked up Joshua's train of thought. "Ned was stepping out with Brianne. But, knowing what a hothead Cheryl was, he protected Brianne by leading Cheryl to believe Angie was the other woman. If Angie found out she was being made a scapegoat, she could have confronted Ned and Brianne."

"Do you happen to remember the cause of Angie's death?" Joshua asked Harry.

"Angie had a fractured skull. However, the ME said it wasn't necessarily bad enough to have killed her. But it was serious enough to have knocked her out long enough to strap her into the front seat of her car and push it off a boat dock into the river. After being in the river for so long, it was difficult for the ME to say conclusively that she had drowned."

Joshua said, "I'd like to have the ME take a second look at Angie Sullivan's body. Forensics have come a long way since 1984. Maybe they can uncover more evidence to point to who killed her."

"Are you thinking that whoever killed Cheryl Smith killed Angie?" Harry asked.

"It's a possibility," Cameron replied. "Cheryl did have over a dozen alibi witnesses."

The retired detective sat forward. "I think it's more likely that one of Angie's friends killed Cheryl to deliver some frontier justice."

"Maybe, maybe not."

Joshua said, "A second look at Angie's body could answer that question for us so we don't have to speculate. Who was the last to see Angie alive?"

"Her fiancé," Harry said, "Kyle Bostwick. They got engaged the very night she disappeared." He sucked in a deep breath. "She still had the ring on her finger when her body was found."

# Chapter Six

"Cheryl Smith? Star? Of anything?" Kyle Bostwick pushed his glasses up on his nose and chuckled. "Are you serious?" He sighed and looked up from his feet to Detective Cameron Gates. "If you're waiting for me to say I'm sorry she's dead, you'll have a long wait."

Kyle Bostwick had been Chester born and raised. After earning his degree in computer programming, he opened a computer sales and repair shop on Carolina Avenue, one block from Joshua's Chester office.

In addition to the prosecutor's office down the river in New Cumberland, Joshua also had an office a few blocks from his house. Preferring to work remotely via his computer, he rarely used either office.

Being a hometown boy, who had taken good care of his widowed mother until her death, Kyle Bostwick had no trouble getting work installing and maintaining computer systems for homes and businesses in the tri-state area. A quick scan of his office indicated that he was all-business. Void of personal items, the shop area was filled with desktop and laptop computers, and other office equipment of every brand, size, and type.

Pale and slightly built, Kyle resembled the stereotype of a computer geek. All that was missing was the plastic pocket protector in the breast pocket of his plaid button-down shirt. His nerdy appearance was compounded by thick eyeglasses over beady eyes that peered out under heavy eyelids.

During their interview, he refused to look directly at Cameron. Instead, he'd look over her shoulder or at the floor. Usually, the detective found such manners during an interview suspicious. With this witness, however, she was relieved to not have Kyle look directly at her. His giant beady eyeballs gave her the creeps.

"You never married," she noted.

"There was only one Angie Sullivan," he said in a firm tone. "She was the love of my life. We were going to get married."

"I'm sorry for your loss," she replied. "I understand how difficult this can be for you to talk about, but can you tell me what happened that night at the skating rink?"

After adjusting his glasses, Kyle eyed the wall behind her. "I already went over this with the police a dozen times years ago. Everyone knows Cheryl killed Angie. I guess it's some sort of twist of fate that the mob would finally give her the justice she deserved."

"That's not for me or you to decide," Cameron said. "Good or bad, someone killed Cheryl Smith, and that someone could have killed a dozen people blowing up Gordon's house to cover up her murder."

"Excuse me if I'm not inclined to cooperate." He plopped down behind his desk and interlocked his fingers together.

She leaned over his desk at him. "And you'll excuse me if I take you over to the police station in Pennsylvania in the back of my cruiser with all of your friends and neighbors watching.

Staring through her, the corners of Kyle's lips curled. "When they find out why, whose side do you think they'll take?"

*Touché.* Cameron opted for another approach. "Cheryl Smith never had a day in court."

"Because she ran off to Hollywood to do what she does best—sex and drugs with rock stars like Mick Jagger after dumping Angie in the river to rot."

"She had an alibi."

"From her low-life friends."

"What if she didn't kill Angie?" She waited for his response.

Kyle's eyes finally met hers.

The sight of his enlarged eyeballs peering out at her from under the heavy eyelids caused a shiver to go down her spine. Under the pretense of examining a new model laptop, she turned away. "Can you think of anyone else who would have wanted to hurt Angie?"

"Everyone loved Angie—except Cheryl Smith."

"What did Cheryl have against her?" Cameron asked.

"Jealousy," Kyle replied. "She had beauty and class, and Cheryl didn't."

"How about Ned Carter?"

"What about Ned Carter?"

"I heard that Angie was sneaking around with Ned behind Cheryl's back? That's what the fight was about."

Kyle's pale face turned pink. "That's a lie!" He almost jumped out of his seat.

The force of her demeanor and the look in her eye was enough to make him back down into his chair. "Then what were they fighting about?"

"I—I don't know."

Cameron was doubtful. "After all these years, you have no idea what Cheryl and Angie were fighting about?"

"It doesn't matter. It was nothing." He took off his glasses and cleaned them with his shirt tail. "I didn't care. Whatever it was, it wasn't important enough for her to take Angie away from me." He put his glasses back on. "Doesn't matter what it was about."

Cameron felt a tug of sympathy in her heart. "How long were you with Angie after leaving the skating rink?"

He shifted in his seat.

"Tell me what happened after the fight."

Kyle stared straight ahead while recounting. "Angie and I met at the Melody Lane Skating Rink when we were sophomores. I went to Oak Glen High School—"

She made a mental note that was the same school Joshua's son Donny was attending. Joshua and all of his children had graduated from Oak Glen.

"—Angie went to South Side High School in Hookstown." He paused. "It was love at first sight. She was my first kiss—my first love. We had it all planned. We were going to West Virginia University in Morgantown. She was going to study nursing. I was going to study computer programming. After our first year, we would get married, and then move out of the dorms into our own apartment. After graduation, we would move back home to Chester, and she would get a job at East Liverpool City Hospital, and I would set up my own computer shop here." He tapped the top of his desk.

"I love a man who knows how to plan." Cameron fought to keep the edge of sarcasm out of her voice. She favored spontaneity, something that Joshua found he admired and feared in her.

"I saved for a year to buy her a diamond ring. I did yard work and mowed like every lawn between here and the state line. I was going to give it to her at the skating rink, where we had met, after the last slow skate, but when I found her, Cheryl and her friends were all over her. By the time I broke it up, the skate was over. So I decided to give it to her down by the river. We had a spot on a bench overlooking the river. We liked to sit and look at the lights and talk … and kiss."

"That was where her car was found in the river."

He nodded. "I couldn't believe it when they found her there … of all places."

"And you were the last one to see her alive."

His eyes met hers. "Oh no, I wasn't."

"Who else was the last one with her?"

"Whoever killed her." His eyes filled with tears. "We were going to get married. We even set a date."

"What date?"

"July 7, 1979."

"So you give her the ring, and she accepts your marriage proposal," Cameron said. "Then what happened?"

His eyes were glassy. "We made love. It was glorious. Unbelievable." He swallowed. "My first and only time. There could never be anyone after Angie."

Cameron's cheeks felt warm at his confession. "Did you see or hear anyone else around who may have seen you?"

"No," he answered before shrugging. "Angie was my whole world. She was the only one in the universe as far as I was concerned."

"What happened after that?"

"She took me home."

She blinked. "*She* took *you* home."

"I didn't—"

"That's right," Cameron said more to herself than him, "it was her car that she was in."

"I was saving all of my money for college. Since Angie had a car, I didn't need one. If I needed a ride, she'd give me one or one of my other friends."

"But then somehow she ended up back at the yacht club, and her car in the river."

"It had to be Cheryl and her friends," Kyle said. "They were down there at the First Street Overlook, right next to the yacht club. They must have been following us."

"Where was she going after taking you home?" Cameron asked.

"Home," Kyle said.

"But she didn't go home."

"Cheryl's scum-bag friends must have kidnapped her," he said.

Opting to get off the merry-go-round she was on, Cameron shifted gears so sharply that she threw Kyle off track. "Did you see Cheryl Smith when she came back to town in 1985?"

"If I had, I would have called the police."

Cameron cocked her head at him with a smile. "Not if you killed her."

"In which case, I wouldn't tell you if I had."

"You worked at Davenport Winery when you first got out of college," she said. "You set up their computer network."

"So?" Kyle replied. "It takes a while to set up a business and get it running. Brianne Davenport was a friend. She helped me out by giving me a job. Davenport Winery is one of my biggest clients. When the Internet came about, I got them set up. I took them worldwide."

"You were working for them in 1985."

"So again?" he scoffed.

"That was when Cheryl came into the area and was killed." Cameron leaned over his desk. "She had the number to Brianne Davenport's direct line in her pocket. Are you sure she didn't come by the winery, and you didn't see her."

"Positive."

She stood up and sauntered to the door. "If I find out you're lying, I'll be back." She turned to him. "If you think you don't like me now, wait until you see me after I found out you'd lied to me."

~ ~ ~ ~

Cameron was huddled over her mini laptop behind Joshua's desk in his study.

His huge body sprawled out across the Oriental rug, Admiral occupied the whole floor space in the middle of the room.

Irving had made himself at home stretched out across the front of the desk behind his mistress's laptop. His head tilted back, his eyes half closed; he looked like he was meditating on the case while Cameron took notes.

"I saw your car out front." Jan stepped over the canine's sleeping body. "What are you doing here?"

In response to Irving's sharp glare, Jan stopped to give him an obligatory scratch behind the ear. Satisfied with the attention tossed his way, he returned to meditating.

"Working." Cameron continued studying the laptop. "Josh had meetings and asked me to stick around to make sure Donny came straight home to study for his science test." She noticed Jan eying the thick manila envelope resting under Irving's front paws.

"What makes him think you'd have any better luck getting Donny to study?" Jan sat down on the sofa and slipped off her shoes.

"I can be very persuasive," Cameron drawled. "I paid him twenty dollars."

"Smart lady."

"Either that or lazy," she said. "I didn't feel like arguing with the kid. He's as strong-willed as his father."

"The Thornton and MacMillan genes are tenacious." Jan smiled while patting her tummy. "I did some research on the Internet about Cherry Pickens, aka Cheryl Smith."

"So did I."

"What if we compare notes?"

"What if we don't?" Cameron refused to look up from the laptop.

Jan got up to move in closer. "What if I discovered something you've missed?"

"I'd doubt it if you did."

"Are you sure about that?" she whispered into her ear.

Catching Jan attempting to read the monitor, Cameron shut the lid to the laptop. "You're the media. That makes you the enemy when it comes to open murder cases."

Placing her hands on her hips, Jan stood up. "Hey! I've been sitting on the story of the century without reporting any of it because of family loyalty. So don't you go calling me the enemy. If I was the enemy, I would have reported that there's reason to believe the lady in the freezer is Cheryl Smith as soon as Tad told me about it."

"After which you would have found yourself sleeping in Admiral's dog house."

"Admiral doesn't have a dog house."

"True," Cameron said.

"The least you can do is let me in on what you've got so I'll be ready when you guys give me the word to run with it."

"You're as tenacious as Tad and Josh. Are you sure you only married into the family? Josh tells me that a case could be made that some families in this valley are inbred."

"That's not true," Jan said in a shrill tone. "I swear I'm going to slip arsenic in his tea for saying that. How about it?"

"Slip arsenic into Josh's tea?" Cameron shook her head. "I don't think so."

"I mean, I'll tell you what I know if you tell me what you know."

Cameron raised an eyebrow in her direction. "It's not obstructing an investigation if I don't tell you what I know. It is if you don't tell me."

"You should give me something in return."

Cameron studied her for a minute. "You don't have anything." She turned back to lift the lid to her laptop, only to find Jan's hand holding it down. The detective sighed. "If I pay you twenty dollars will you go away?"

"When Cherry Pickens left Vegas—when she disappeared—she was driving a red Ferrari 308 GTS."

"That's a really bitching car," Cameron said.

Even Irving seemed to take notice. He opened his emerald-green eyes to peer over at Jan. One of his black ears with white tufts cocked in her direction. His tail twitched.

"Yes, it is," Jan said. "Not the average pickup truck you see around these parts. My question is, if Cherry Pickens was Cheryl Smith, and she came back here to get murdered, then what happened to the car?"

The two women exchanged glances.

She could have ditched the car before landing in Hookstown," Cameron said.

"What if she didn't?"

"Then there could be the motive for her murder," Cameron muttered. "I'm impressed, Jan." She lifted the lid to her laptop.

"Impressed with what?" Wearing his winter coat and carrying his briefcase, Joshua came in. He stopped when he saw Irving stretched out across his desk. "What is *that* doing on my desk?"

Irving directed his glare at him. His tail twitched like a fencer's foil. He almost seemed to say, "Yeah, I'm using your desk for my afternoon nap. What do you intend to do about it?"

"He's my muse," Cameron said. "He helps me focus."

"He also sheds." Joshua set his briefcase next to the desk.

Wounded by the observation, Irving jumped down. With a glance over his shoulder at Joshua, he stuck his tail straight up into the air and hitched his rear end up in his direction before stalking out of the study.

"I think you just got the feline version of the finger," Jan said.

"He does that to me all the time."

Jan said, "I thought Irving liked you."

"He did," he replied.

"And then what?" she asked. "What did you do to him?"

"I did nothing." Clutching his chest, he backed up a step.

"Joshua slept with his woman," Cameron told her.

Jan turned to him. "Home wrecker."

Joshua fought the blush rising to his cheeks. Judging by the grin that came to Jan's lips, he knew his childhood friend saw his embarrassment. "Irving can find someone in his own species."

"No, he can't," Cameron said. "He's been fixed. I was it."

"Then I guess he's going to have to get over it." Joshua went to his next concern. "I hope you two aren't working together."

"No," Cameron said, "Jan's just bugging me."

"Stop bugging her," Joshua ordered.

"What's that?" Jan indicated the envelope that Irving had been guarding.

Cameron laid her hand flat on it. "None of your business."

The gesture confirming her suspicion, she pounced. "Is that the autopsy report on Cheryl Smith? Is it official?"

Cameron glanced up at Joshua, who slowly nodded his head. "It's official. It is Cheryl Anne Smith, aka Cherry Pickens."

"What was the cause of death?" Jan reached for the envelope which the detective slid out of her reach.

"Broken neck," Joshua said.

"Could it have been an accident?" she asked.

"Right," Cameron smiled. "She got high on heroin and had an accident, broke her neck, then she crawled into that freezer, and died."

"Did you say heroin?" Jan asked.

Cameron was equally coy when she answered, "Yep, the same drug used to kill Blake Norton, the pop star Cherry Pickens was fooling around with while Humphrey Phoenix was financing her boob job. He was found tied up in a chair and with a needle in his arm."

Jan wondered out loud, "If Cherry knew about Phoenix killing her boyfriend, she had to have known that she'd be next. That's why she came back here, and probably explains who killed her and stuffed her in that freezer."

Cameron was shaking her head. "Nah, this wasn't a professional hit."

Jan was offended by her lack of agreement. "How can you be so sure?"

"Experience," the detective said. "This case has none of the earmarks of a professional hit."

Joshua agreed. "Albert had no mob ties. And if he did, he had thirty years to get rid of the body so it would never be found. That tells me he didn't know it was there." He turned to Cameron. "That business card found in her back pocket. It had the phone number to Brianne Davenport's direct line. She wouldn't give that number to just anyone."

"If I was on the run," Jan noted, "I'd be more likely to run to my ex-boyfriend than his wife. Cherry used to be hot and heavy with Ned Carter." She asked the detective, "Have you interviewed him yet?"

"She had his car phone number written on the back of the business card," Cameron said. "But think about it. Cheryl's on the run. What do you need most when you're on the run?

Money to run with. Where was she more likely to get some? One of the richest women in the tri-state area."

"Unless you had a drug habit and needed a fix," Joshua mused. "Ned Carter did dabble in drugs back when she knew him. Managing the casino and track, he has connections; which, according to rumors, he still keeps in touch with."

"But you need money to buy a fix," Cameron pointed out.

"Ned Carter has both," Joshua pointed out. "He's got the connections to take care of her fix, and the rich wife from whom he can get the cash to give her to run with."

"I love a man with the power of deductive reasoning," she said in a husky voice.

# Chapter Seven

Cameron drove up the winding hill to the Davenport estate. The sprawling white farmhouse resembled a southern plantation home built into the side of a steep hill. Vineyards cascaded down the front of the estate to the peasants' farms hidden among deep woods beneath the hundred-year-old antebellum-style house. The original home had been added onto again and again until it became the biggest along Snowden Road.

Making her way up the long twisting drive, the thick woods gave way to rows of grapevines, one row above the other until the driveway leveled off at the floral gardens that surrounded the house.

Acreage-wise, Doris Sullivan's horse farm, Sullivan Stables, located on the other side of the country road, was bigger than the Davenport estate. Grandeur-wise, the winery had everyone beat.

"I have a feeling we're not in Chester anymore, Irving," Cameron told the skunk cat in the passenger seat of her cruiser.

Irving let out a mixture between a growl and a meow upon sighting a squirrel racing out of a flower bed and up a maple tree.

"If she's such a debutante," Cameron muttered in a low voice to the cat, "Then what's she doing here in Hookstown? Why isn't she on some reality show chasing some teen pop star?" She pulled the Pennsylvania State Police cruiser around to park in front of the wrap-around porch. "This place is big." Concluding her skunk cat would not be welcome inside the mansion, Cameron delegated Irving to guarding the cruiser while she went inside to interview Brianne Davenport.

A housekeeper named Harriet answered the door. After studying the detective's gold police shield, the older woman showed her into the foyer with the pleasantness of a friend. "What makes a woman want to become a homicide detective?"

"I wanted to meet men." Cameron was admiring the high ceilings and luxurious decor of the foyer. She forced herself to keep her chin from her knees while she took in the antiques and classic style of the furnishings.

Harriett invited her into the living room to show off the garden that started at the end of the patio. The entire northern side of the house was made up of windows to take in the trees, fountains, statues, and a garage the size of a middle-class home on the far side of back yard. In the distance, Cameron could make out another vineyard that stretched to the far tree line.

"You can wait here," Harriet told her. "Ms. Davenport will be right with you."

Several minutes after the housekeeper left her, Cameron heard a door open and shut down a hallway before footsteps galloped in her direction. A young man who looked only a few years older than Donny slid to a halt when he saw the detective, her hand on her gun, in the room.

His long, blond hair fell straight to his shoulders. His soft face was flushed down to his chest. In contrast to his effeminate face, his broad shoulders and chest was muscular. "Oh," he said upon seeing her.

"Oh," she replied. "Who are you?"

As if he didn't know how to answer, he paused before answering. "I'm Freddie." His eyes never left her face.

Cameron felt like she was looking into the face of a department store mannequin. All looks, but hollow inside. She didn't know who Freddie was, but she had already determined that he wasn't very bright.

"Are you really a cop?"

"That's why they give me the gold shield." *Who is this guy?*

Carrying a stack of sealed envelopes, Harriet came back into the room. "Freddie, Brianne asked that you take these party invitations to the post office. She wants them post marked today. Could you also wash the Mercedes? She'll be driving that to the McDonald party tonight."

"Later, detective." He rushed out to the foyer.

"Cameron, how good of you to come!" Brianne Davenport bound into the room and up to her with a wide grin on her face. A waft of perfume combined with a musky scent came into the room with her. Her pink cheeks and bright eyes left little to the detective's imagination about what she had been doing during her meeting with Freddie. Brianne ushered the detective to the sofa where they sat down.

"I didn't mean to upset your …" Cameron began their interview with an apology.

"My what?"

"Meeting."

"Oh, you mean Freddie." She cast Cameron a wicked grin. "That's perfectly fine. Freddie and I will finish later, I assure you."

"How does your husband feel about that?" Cameron asked.

"What he doesn't know—"

"Still hurts him," she finished.

Brianne's eyes narrowed to slits. "Did you come to give me unsolicited marriage counseling or to talk about that bomb in Albert Gordon's basement?"

"I came to talk to you about Cheryl Smith."

Brianne batted her thick eyelashes. "Who?" It came out as a high-pitched squawk that was not befitting to her sultry image.

"Someone from your past," Cameron explained, "who we found hidden in that basement where the bomb was planted." She cocked her head at her and narrowed her eyes. "Don't tell me you don't know Cheryl Smith."

"A lifetime ago," Brianne said. "She *used* to be my friend."

"Really?"

"Until she destroyed and killed my best friend."

"That friend being …"

"Angie Sullivan." Sadness filled Brianne's flawless face. Confusion took over. "Wait a minute. Cheryl Smith was hiding in Albert's basement?"

"Cheryl Smith's *body* was found stuffed in a freezer in Albert Gordon's basement."

Brianne scoffed. "You know Albert Gordon was the one who got the judge to give Cheryl permission to take off after she killed Angie. I didn't speak to him for years after he did that."

"Were you mad enough to kill her and hide her body in Gordon's basement to make some sort of statement—only to have him not notice it to get the point?"

Brianne cocked her head. "Do you mean, instead of Cheryl running off, someone killed her and hid her body in her lawyer's house?"

Cameron explained about Cheryl Smith changing her identity and becoming an actress in sex movies before returning to the area and getting killed. "Did you see her when she came back here?"

"No way," Brianne replied. "I hated her for what she did to Angie. She knew that if I laid eyes on her, I would have called the cops."

"How did she know that?"

"I told her," Brianne said. "When Angie disappeared, everyone knew Cheryl killed her. But the police didn't have anything because her warped friends gave her an alibi. So they couldn't arrest her. I let her know, we all let her know—"

"We being who?" Cameron asked.

"Me, Ned, Kyle, all of Angie's friends—that we were all watching her, and if we got anything …" She paused. "I guess it worked too well because a couple of weeks later Cheryl was flying off to California, and there was nothing anybody could do to stop her."

Cameron recalled her saying that she and Cheryl used to be friends.

"Cheryl, Angie, and I used to hang out together … until high school when Cheryl blossomed and got popular with the boys. Then it went to her head. She thought she ruled the world until Ned—"

"Your husband Ned?"

"That's right. My husband Ned took a liking to Angie, who never did anything to anyone." Her eyes fell to her feet. "But he never acted on it. Angie had no idea, but Cheryl saw it. She was bound and determined to make Angie pay, even though she never did anything to encourage him."

"How did she decide to make her pay?"

Brianne replied with silence.

Their eyes met.

Cameron repeated her question.

Brianne sighed. "There was a big age difference between Doris Sullivan and Angie."

"How big of a difference?" the detective asked.

"Seventeen years." She explained, "Back when Angie was born, girls who had babies out of wedlock were considered … you know. So, when Doris got pregnant, she went to live with an aunt down in Wheeling. Then, when she had Angie, they pretended she was Doris' younger sister. Somehow, Cheryl found out and told everyone."

"Doris was secretly Angie's mother." Cameron pieced it together. "Did Angie know before Cheryl told her?"

"Yes, Angie knew. Doris told her after her parents, I mean grandparents, were killed in that car accident. Angie was cool with it, until Cheryl and her friends spread it all over, especially when they ganged up on her at the skating rink that night."

"I guess by that time the friendship was over and done with," the detective said.

"Oh, yeah."

"When Angie disappeared, did you tell the police detective about Cheryl spilling the Sullivans family secret?"

"No, of course not." Brianne shook her head with a loud gasp. "Doris was upset enough about Angie disappearing. When Cheryl first started spreading it around, Angie begged us all to keep quiet about it so Doris wouldn't know. She didn't want her sister—mother hurt. When Angie disappeared, we talked about it—me, Ned, and Kyle, and everyone else who had heard it—and we vowed not to let Doris find out."

Cameron cleared her throat. "Which could have directly interfered with the detective's investigation into Angie's disappearance."

"How?" Brianne's eyes narrowed and her mouth dropped open in a scoff. "Cheryl killing Angie years later had nothing to do with Doris getting knocked up when she was a teenager."

"How do you know that?"

Brianne's eye rolled up to the ceiling and across the room in the same manner as the adolescent men she adored.

"Well," Cameron said, "you kept this information a secret before. Why are you telling me about it now?"

"To let you know exactly how much of a witch Cheryl was," Brianne replied. "She deserved exactly what she got." Under Cameron's questioning gaze, she added, "But she didn't get it from me."

"If you did, I'll find out."

"Don't be so certain of that," Brianne challenged her.

When her host started to stand up to escort her out, Cameron said, "I have a few more questions."

"Then get on with it." Brianne sat back on the sofa.

Cameron showed her a copy of the business card found in Cheryl Smith's pocket with her direct line phone number on it. "Am I correct in assuming that you don't freely give that number out?"

Brianne slowly shook her head and tucked a loose lock of dark hair behind her ear. "When was she killed?"

"Summer of 1985."

"I have no idea how she ended up with that phone number." She suggested, "I give my business cards out to a lot of people. Someone must have given it to her."

"Then you deny seeing her and giving this to her?"

"I haven't spoken to Cheryl Smith since that night at the Melody Lane Skating Rink, which is when she killed Angie."

"But didn't you just tell me that you told her *after* Angie disappeared that you'd call the police if you ever laid eyes on her once they got proof that she killed Angie?"

Brianne's mouth became tight.

"How did you tell her that *after* Angie's disappearance if you never spoke to her since that night at the skating rink?" Cameron smirked. She had tripped her up.

"I meant since Cheryl left town *after* Angie disappeared."

"Fair enough," Cameron said. "You were eighteen years old when Cheryl Smith took off for Hollywood. Your father was running the winery at that time." She showed her the copy of the business card. "This lists your name as owner, which you became in 1983 *after* your father's death, *before* Davenport Winery expanded and went public in the 1990's. This business card was made up *after* Cheryl went to Hollywood. Do you have any idea how she got it?"

"No."

"How about your husband?"

Brianne scoffed. "Ned? He hated Cheryl more than I did."

"But he was her boyfriend at one point."

"In high school, and only because she put out."

"There was another number on this card—on the back." Cameron held up the paper for her to read. "Your husband's car phone number."

Brianne's eyes widened. Her face grew pale. "You'll have to ask him about that."

"I will." Cameron folded up the paper, and put it back in her pocket. "What were you doing at Albert Gordon's house?"

Brianne's eyes widened at the question. "What?"

"What were you doing at Albert Gordon's house on the day of the explosion?"

"Same as everyone else," she replied. "I was helping to clean it out. I hired the caterer, who's mad as hell at me since he lost his truck. Don't you remember?"

Cameron nodded her head. "Yes, I remember you being there. My question is why were you there? The volunteers were all members of the Albert's church, to whom he had left the farm and his estate. You don't belong to that group."

"Neither do you," she countered.

"I was invited by Joshua Thornton," Cameron said, "Albert's cousin—to help his family." She cocked her head. "I still can't figure out why you were there. You don't strike me as the type who gets into doing hard, physical, dirty work. How well did you know Albert?"

"He and my father were fishing buddies," Brianne said. "And as for why I was there—*Joshua* invited me."

"Joshua? My Joshua?"

"*My* Joshua." Brianne smirked. "Any more questions?"

"No." Cameron stood up. "I'm through here." She got halfway across the room before turning around.

Brianne was smirking like a schoolgirl, who just got one over on the nerd.

"One more thing." Cameron stepped up to her. "Don't ever lie to me again. Because that makes me mad—seriously mad. It's not a good idea to get a woman who carries a police shield—and a gun—seriously mad at you—because you're very liable to get seriously hurt. Understand?"

The color drained from Brianne's face. Her eyes narrowed to slits. "Understood."

"Stay away from Donny. He's not into older women."

Brianne's attractive features dissolved. Her face hardened with determination. "I have yet to meet a young man who's not into older women, especially when that older woman is me."

# CHAPTER EIGHT

"Has the board made any decision yet about Albert's replacement as church elder," Doris asked Joshua while his mouth was filled with runny scrambled eggs.

*I wish I was someplace more pleasant right now—like in Tad's morgue watching him perform an autopsy.*

It was the Rotary Club's weekly breakfast meeting at the Mountaineer Resort in Newell. The meal was served as a buffet, which Joshua despised anyway. Resting under the heat lamps, the food resembled leftovers to him. Cameron claimed he was spoiled after years of eating meals cooked by his daughter Tracy, a gourmet cook.

Her plate loaded with scrambled eggs and biscuits drenched in sausage gravy, Doris Sullivan took the seat across from Joshua to make a case for her taking Albert Gordon's position on the church's board of elders.

Such a position was coveted. Often, it was inherited, a coincidence that was purely unintentional. Joshua's grandfather had been an elder and, upon his death, his wife took his spot. In the early 1970's, a woman being given such a position was a big deal. Tad took Frieda Thornton's place on the board after she had passed away. As soon as he moved back to

Chester, Joshua was offered a newly created seat, even though he had been gone for over twenty years. Somehow, it only seemed right.

Such positions were quietly offered by the pastor or other elders from behind the scenes. However, both Doris Sullivan and Mildred Hildebrand had launched into what resembled a full-fledge campaign to take Albert's place on the board—complete with negative advertising.

At first, Joshua welcomed the change of topic from Cherry Pickens' body being found in his cousin's basement. While the identity of the lady in the freezer wasn't public knowledge, enough people knew about it to make the murder a hot topic for speculation. The murder case was growing in fame with every day that passed without a statement from the lead investigator, who happened to be the girlfriend of the cousin of the homeowner whose basement in which the body had been stashed. Accusations of a cover-up were being whispered. They were running out of time.

"Were you aware that Mildred Hildebrand has high blood pressure?" Doris sprinkled salt over her eggs and biscuits before tasting it. "This is only my opinion, but it really wouldn't do to select an elder who's likely to have a stroke at any time. At my last physical, the doctor told me that I have the body of a twenty-five year old. I'm still down in the barn at six o'clock every morning feeding the horses and cleaning stalls. I haven't had a cold in over forty years."

"When it comes to serving as church elder," Joshua said, "spiritual maturity is more important than physical health."

He fought to keep his attention focused on Doris when he spied Brianne across the room working her charms on a handsome server who looked to still be in college. Not far away, Ned Carter had also noticed his wife rubbing her hand up and down the server's biceps.

"I understand Cheryl Smith was a chief suspect in your sister's murder." Joshua refrained from mentioning the rumor about Angie being Doris' daughter. In all the years that he had known Doris, he had never heard about it. That made him think it was an ugly, juvenile rumor. Even if it was true, it was still a family secret, which he didn't want to mention unless forced to since Doris had lost the last member of her family.

Doris started at the abrupt change of subject. "Everyone knows Cheryl killed her."

"But she had an alibi," Joshua replied.

"Her lying friends." Doris cast her eyes on him. "I got a call from the Hancock County sheriff's office. He says you want to dig up Angie's body and have another autopsy done."

"I think you should do it."

"Why should I?"

"What if Cheryl didn't kill her?" he asked.

"Who else would have?" she replied.

"I don't know," Joshua said. "But forensics has come a long, long way since 1984. If it was one of my kids, and there was any chance that I was wrong about who killed them, I'd want to know it."

"They want to disturb her grave," she said with tears in her eyes.

"I'm sure she won't mind if it helps to catch her killer."

Doris' lips pulled together. "Are they sure it was Cheryl's body in Albert's basement?"

"Definitely."

"How'd she get there?"

"Someone stuffed her in a freezer and hid it in the basement, the same basement where the bomb that could have killed a dozen people had been planted."

She blinked at Joshua. When his eyes met hers, she clutched her chest. "You certainly don't think I planted that bomb."

"You were the last one down in the basement before it was discovered. That freezer contained the body of the prime suspect in your sister's murder. If the blast had destroyed the freezer and body—"

Doris snorted. "A lot of people went down into the basement that morning including Mildred and her daughter Gail."

"Why would they have planted that bomb?"

"Gail Hildebrand hated Cheryl Smith as much as anyone," she said. "Cheryl and her friends were abusive to her."

"How were they abusive?" Joshua looked around the banquet room until he spotted the topic of their conversation.

The owner of a marketing agency, Gail Hildebrand was a fixture at all of the business networking organizations in the area. Her agency was under contract with the Mountaineer Resort.

Joshua spotted her talking to the casino manager, Ned Carter. When they saw the prosecutor watching them, they turned around and left the banquet room.

*What is that about?*

"Bullying," Doris was saying. "Gail is nothing like her mother, except for her voluptuous figure. She was plump when she was a young girl. But the way Cheryl and his friends teased her, you would have thought she was an elephant. She was the best skater at the rink. And a talented baton twirler, too. Cheryl about ruined her youth with her bullying."

Joshua noted, "But when Cheryl's body was discovered, she had a business card with Brianne Davenport's private line in her pocket, not Gail's. Do you have any idea why?"

"How should I know? It was Brianne's phone number, not mine."

❧ ❧ ❧ ❧

While the Mountaineer Resort catered mostly to wealthy business people, gamblers, and other transient types that hung around the race track and casino, Ned Carter was a businessman through and through.

Decorated in brass and mirrors, the sight of the VIP lounge located on the top floor of the resort took Cameron back to less than happy times. Behind the bar stretching the length of the lounge, bottles of every type of booze imaginable were begging to be tipped to fill the shiny glasses that hung from the rack above. She felt blessed that those times consisted of only a few years after her husband's sudden death. She had spiraled to hit her bottom fast in order to rebound back to sobriety and regain everything that she had lost. She knew too many whose rock-bottom was much lower than hers and would never be able to regain their losses.

The detective tried not to make eye contact with the two men who made their home on stools at the end of the bar. Between sips of their liquid lunch served in short glasses, they lifted their heads bowed over their drinks and cigarettes to admire the slender woman detective with wavy, cinnamon-colored hair. She didn't have to tell them that she was a detective. They could see that in the police shield she wore on her utility belt along with her gun, radio, and baton.

When Cameron asked for Ned, the bartender looked her up and down until her eyes landed on the gold shield. Then, she hurried back into the office to fetch her boss.

From behind the office door, Cameron heard a familiar woman's voice, which she couldn't place, before the bartender interrupted to announce a police detective was there to see Ned.

"What about?" a man's voice demanded to know.

"Don't know," the bartender responded.

"Wait here," he ordered someone, "and keep quiet."

The bartender closed the door on her way out before the manager slipped out of the office to face the detective.

Having seen a picture of Cherry forever frozen in her youth, Cameron half-expected to find a man in roughly the same condition; young and viral. Maybe even with a head of shaggy hair and a muscular chest.

Ned Carter wasn't as lucky as Cheryl Smith. His slender body showed signs of effort to maintain his shape with exercise, but his hair had not cooperated. The top was thinning and the skin around his neck sagged. The formerly lean ladies' man compensated for the loss of his youthful good looks with expensive suits and shiny buffed nails.

"Are you Ned Carter?"

Ned studied the slender, attractive woman before him, dressed in slightly faded jeans with an expensive leather jacket over a red sweater. "I guess you're the detective that's been asking about Cheryl Smith. Brianne told me about you. I'll make this quick. The last time I saw Cheryl was the day before she flew off to California. Did I kill her? No. Did I want to? Yes."

When he turned away, she called him back. "Witnesses tell us that she used to be close friends with you. Real close."

"Used to be." Ned directed his attention at the bartender who had moved down the bar to escape the conversation.

Cameron followed Ned when he tried to step away. "But she came back here, and someone killed her."

Ned chuckled. "It wasn't me. A lot of people wanted her dead. You want a list? It's a long one."

"Besides you, who's at the top of that list?" She flashed her most charming grin at Ned's slip.

"Kyle Bostwick," the resort manager said.

"Cheryl didn't have Kyle's phone number in her pocket."

"She didn't need it. Kyle lives in the same house where he was born." Ned grinned. "Did Kyle tell you that Cheryl broke him and Angie up?"

Cameron cocked her head at his wicked smile. "No. Did the original investigator in Angie's case know that?"

"I doubt it," Ned said. "Everyone was concentrating on Cheryl killing her. Besides, Kyle says Angie and him made up and got engaged that night."

"When did they break up?"

"Right before senior prom," Ned recalled. "But they did make up for prom, though Brianne told me that Angie had said it was only because they broke up too late for either of them to get other dates."

"But Cheryl broke them up. How?"

"Oldest game in the book," Ned said. "Cheryl was hot and put out. Angie was as pure as the driven snow and insisted on staying that way until her wedding night. Cheryl flashed her boobs at Kyle and he crumbled. Then Cheryl …" he grumbled, "recorded the whole thing and sent the tape to Angie. She was devastated and broke up with him."

Cameron nodded her head while imagining the pain that Cheryl Smith had caused during her short lifetime. "Angie must have forgiven him since she accepted his ring that night."

Ned said, "Only because she didn't have the energy to deal with him right then after what Cheryl had just put her through."

Cameron was aware of the two men at the end of the bar watching and listening to them. They rose up on their haunches in preparation to forcibly evict her if they had to.

She leaned across the bar. "Do you still keep in contact with your old friends?"

"What friends?" Ned asked even though the tone of her voice and arch of her eyebrow told him what she was talking about.

"I understand you used to deal," she answered. "In a place like this, having such connections can come in mighty handy with a certain type of clientele."

"I don't run that type of establishment," Ned answered.

"So I guess you couldn't get hold of say … heroin."

"No."

"Then if Cheryl had contacted you, her connection back in the old days, to ask for a fix, you wouldn't have been able to help her?"

"Oh," Ned said with a wicked grin, "if she had a brain in her head, she'd know that I'd fix her up real good, and not in a good way."

"I think that's what you did," she said. "Cheryl had your phone number in her possession when she died. She called you. You sold or gave her a fix. Then, you even did a roll in the hay for old time's sake—"

"No way," he replied with a threatening edge in his voice.

"Care to give us a DNA sample to prove you didn't?"

"You come back with a warrant, and I'll give you everything you want."

"I'll do that," she told him. "If you were with her, if you sweated on her, if you sneezed on her, then forensics will trace it back to you. So if you did see or talk to her when she came back to town, you better tell me the truth now."

His tan face paled.

"Albert Gordon lived down the road from you," Cameron said. "You saw enough to see that he was a hoarder, so you broke in when he was out of town on a case and hid the freezer in his basement where you knew he'd never find it."

While Ned chuckled in a show of confidence, there was nervousness in his eyes.

"What was Cheryl doing here in Chester?" she asked. "Why'd she come back here when she was on the run? Why didn't she run off to Mexico or Canada? What brought her back here?"

"I'm sure you saw the thing on television about her and Blake Norton, the singer who got offed in Vegas for fooling around with her after the owner of that skin magazine had poured a bunch of money into her." He pointed a finger at Cameron. "That's who killed her. Humphrey Phoenix had her offed. His men followed her here."

"I guess she should have ditched the Ferrari sooner."

"Yeah," Ned agreed.

Cameron cocked her head at him. "Do you know where she ditched it?"

Ned shook his head. "How would I know that if I never saw her or the car?"

"Come on, Ned," she demurred, "You and Cheryl used to be tight. She needed your help. She needed to ditch the car, and she needed a fix. You were the man best able to help her."

"Way back in the old days," he replied with an angry glare. "Not anymore."

"*Assuming* you're telling the truth about not helping her, where would you have sent her *if* she had come to you?"

"If she had come to me, I would have sent her packing for the border and told her to not look back."

"Unfortunately, she obviously didn't do that fast enough because she ended up dead on ice."

The interview over, Cameron crossed the lounge and went out the door, before slipping back to the doorway to peer inside. As she had expected, the woman hiding in Ned's office revealed herself.

*I thought that voice sounded familiar.* Cameron congratulated herself when she saw that it belonged to one of the women helping to clean out Albert's home, Gail Hildebrand.

~ ~ ~ ~

"You're going to get yourself into trouble," Joshua warned Brianne.

"Whatever do you mean?" she asked.

He followed her when she left the dining room to a quiet corner in the lounge where the windows looked out onto the snow-covered courtyard. He wanted to have it out with her. He wondered at how, even though they were married, she and Ned hadn't sat together at the meeting. Even though they were both at the same breakfast meeting, they had barely spoken a word to each other.

"I mean you groping that server while your husband is standing six feet away."

"Ned's and my marriage isn't like most people's." She moved in closer while he backed away. "Why do you keep backing away from me, Josh? Don't you like me?"

"Not really."

"Why did you follow me then?"

"I want to talk to you … about Cheryl Smith."

"Very well." She sat down on the love seat and patted the cushion next to her as an invitation for him to sit with her. "I won't bite. I promise."

Hesitant, Joshua sat down on the love seat, but left a lot of space between them. "Who else Cheryl hurt before going off to Hollywood?"

"Darling, I've pulled the car around."

They both started when they became aware that they weren't alone. Joshua whirled in his seat to look over his shoulder.

Freddie had come into the lounge and came to an abrupt halt when he saw that Brianne was with another man. Uncomfortably aware of an audience, Joshua shifted in his seat to put even more space between them.

"I'll be there in a few minutes, hon. Wait for me outside." She turned her attention to Joshua. "You're talking about a long list."

Joshua said, "But none of them have your phone number."

"I'm not the only one who gives out my business cards," she whispered. "If Cheryl showed up at the business office at the winery and claimed to be a friend of mine, the receptionist would have given her my business card, which had my direct line number. That's how she could have gotten that card."

"And Ned's car phone number?"

"A lot of people have Ned's number. He's a workaholic. People are calling him day and night. That's why I have hobbies."

"Dangerous hobbies."

She reached out to touch his hand. "Don't knock it until you've try it."

He backed away.

"Do I look like a killer to you?" Her hand was on his leg.

Firmly, he put her hand back into her lap and held it there. "Killers come in all shapes and sizes."

Her bottom lip stuck out in a pout. "I don't think you like me."

"Judging by the type of men I've seen you with, I think I'm too old for you."

"I like variety in my men." She leaned toward him and let out a breathy sigh. "Do you really suspect me of killing Cheryl?"

"Considering that your ex-best friend, who was a prime suspect in the murder of your other best friend, was found in a freezer in the basement of a house less than a half mile from yours, with your business card in her pocket, it would be hard *not* to suspect you."

"Do *you* suspect me, Josh?" She moved in closer.

"Yes." He stood up and went around behind the love seat to put it between them.

"Are you afraid of your girlfriend?" she asked. "I should let you know that she threatened me. She flat out told me to stay away from you and your son, or she was going to cause me trouble."

"I'd listen to her if I were you," Joshua said. "Cameron never bluffs."

❧ ❧ ❧ ❧

Outside of the lounge, Doris Sullivan watched Brianne and Joshua whispering to each other. She was startled when Mildred Hildebrand asked her in a loud voice, "Have you heard the news, Doris?"

She whirled around and forced a smile to cross her face. "What news is that, Mildred?"

"I'm now a great-grandmother!" the elderly woman announced with pride. "The count is now three daughters, a son, twelve grandchildren, and one great-grandson. It's a good thing that I'm as organized as I am, or I would never be able to remember all their birthdays and anniversaries." She sighed, "I guess all those years of chairing every board and charity in town has prepared me for managing my growing family … and now position of elder at the church."

"Joshua told me that they haven't made a decision on that yet," Doris said.

"Maybe not, but it's only a matter of time. After all, I've served every other position in the church."

A wicked grin crossed Doris' face. "I think it's wonderful that you're a great-grandmother. You look like one."

"So do you," Mildred responded to the insult. "Unfortunately for you, you can't ever become one at this point. Such a pity."

The two elderly women were eyeing each other when Cameron stepped between them. "Good morning, ladies. How are we today? Have either of you seen Joshua?"

Both women glanced in the direction of the lounge.

Cameron followed their eyes. The corners of her lips curled and a devilish glint came to her eyes. She stepped into the room.

Sensing a cat fight, Doris and Mildred rushed to the doorway to watch.

Joshua saw Brianne's eyes widen with surprise, and a hint of fear. He turned around just in time for his lips to collide with Cameron's. She wrapped her arms around his shoulders to take him into a tight hug. With her mouth on his, she tasted his mouth with an intensity that she had never done before in a public setting. The grip of the gun she wore on her hip dug into his hipbone, but he didn't mind. His head was swimming when she released him. He took a deep breath. "What was that for?"

"That was for nothing." Gazing into his blue eyes, she ran her fingers through his silver hair from the top of his head down past his ears and across his cheeks. "Now you have a license to do something."

"You don't have to tell me twice." He kissed her again.

Disappointed, Mildred and Doris stepped away.

With a glare, Brianne left in search of Freddie.

# Chapter Nine

Irving sat up on his hind legs, with his front paws on the door, to peer out the passenger window when Cameron pulled her cruiser into Raccoon State Park. The skunk cat let out a mixture of a growl and meow from deep in his throat. His emerald eyes widened. His mouth dropped open, and he let out a clicking noise that meant he had something in his sights that he dearly wanted to capture.

The predator was on point.

"Easy going, kiddo," Cameron urged him after unclipping her seat belt before reaching over to unclip Irving's pet seat belt. When she opened the car door, Irving shot out over her lap, scurried under the cruiser and practically flew into the woods.

"They told me you had a skunk for a partner," a deep, male voice boomed from the picnic area. "I didn't believe them."

"Irving is a cat." Cameron sauntered across the gravel parking area to where a huge man was seated on top of the picnic table.

He was dressed in khaki pants and a heavy ski-jacket to protect against the cutting winter wind. While watching her approach him, he took a deep sip of his soda.

"He only looks like a skunk," she said. "You should see the reaction of violent suspects when they see him coming. It's more effective than a K-9."

"Sounds like the reaction of suspects when they see me coming." With a chuckle, he stuck out his hand for her to shake. "Special Investigator William Walton." After shaking her hand, he flashed his FBI identification at her. "Everyone calls me Big Will."

"Detective Cameron Gates." She opened her coat to show him the badge she wore clipped next to her gun on her belt. "They call me a lot of things."

"Sassy. I like that." Big Will chuckled again. "My people say you were asking about a mob contract out on an actress—" He put up his fingers to simulate quotation marks when he used the word "actress". "—named Cherry Pickens that was put out on her in Spring 1985."

"Was it Humphrey Phoenix?" she asked. "I've been told two different things. One said it was the mob, but then I read that Humphrey kept claiming to be a legitimate business man who dealt in smut."

"Correct on both fronts." Standing up, Big Will stuck his thumbs into the waistband of his pants.

Now that he stood to his full height, Cameron saw that Big Will was bigger than she had thought. He towered over her, and was as solid as a tank with muscle. *He wasn't kidding. If I saw him coming at me, I'd be scared, too.*

"Did your check bring up the murder of a has-been pop singer named Blake Norton?" Big Will asked. "He was in Vegas trying to make a comeback."

Nodding, Cameron took up the story. "Cherry Pickens was fooling around with him behind Phoenix's back. So he had Blake Norton killed and put out a contract on Cherry Pickens. That's why she disappeared."

Big Will grinned. "Phoenix didn't want Pickens killed. He only wanted to send her a message by killing Norton."

"Then why did she run?"

"The hit was carried out by a couple of mob assassins. While Phoenix didn't work with the mob, he did have powerful friends and connections. Those powerful friends contracted the hit as a favor, but things went wrong." He paused for dramatic effect. "Cherry Pickens was hiding in the bathroom."

"That made her a witness," Cameron said.

"No matter how much money Phoenix had invested in Cherry Pickens, the mob couldn't let her live to tell. Somehow, she managed to escape, which says a lot considering that these were pros. That was when the contract was adjusted to include her … for damage control."

"But she had escaped."

Big Will smiled. "Like I said, she was a resourceful girl. You got to be good to be able to escape not just the scene, but the town when you have the mob after you—especially in Vegas." Looking down at her, he folded his arms across his chest. "Now tell me about your interest in Cherry Pickens."

"We found her body."

"Where?"

"In a freezer in the basement of a hoarder house in Hookstown," she said. "The house happened to belong to the lawyer who had done some work for her several years before."

Big Will's eyes widened. His mouth dropped open slightly. "I don't suppose COD was natural causes."

"Broken neck. She had a high amount of heroin in her system. She probably would have OD'd if her neck wasn't snapped." She went on to ask the question she had contacted the FBI to ask. "Is there any possibility that this was a mob hit?"

"Did the hoarder have any mob ties?"

"None."

"When was she killed?"

"We pinpointed the date to the summer of 1985," she said.

"She disappeared in early May 1985, when Blake Norton was killed." Big Will scratched his head. "So she was killed a few weeks later."

"That's what it looks like," Cameron said. "Do your people know if anyone ever took credit for hitting her? Did anyone collect on it?"

"No way that was a mob hit," Big Will said with certainty. "In 1989, an informant, who is now in the witness protection program, reported that the mob still had a contract out on Cherry Pickens."

"Which means the motive for her murder was something else," Cameron said.

"That's what it looks like to me." Big Will sniffed and looked around.

When a foul odor reached her nose, Cameron covered her face. She could hear Irving screeching behind her.

Big Will covered his face with one hand while pointing over her shoulder with the other. "I thought you said that was a cat."

Whirling around, Cameron saw Irving racing across the parking lot toward her. His fur was flared so that he looked twice his size. As he grew closer, the stench became worse. "Irving? Is that you?"

"Skunk!" Big Will turned to run. In his hysteria, he banged into the edge of the picnic table and fell over. He rolled before scrambling to his feet and running up the hill to where his car was parked along the road.

Cameron wanted to back away also, but she couldn't leave Irving, who was equally hysterical. When he got to her, he stopped, dropped, rolled, and pawed at his face with first one paw and then the other.

"What did you do?"

Irving howled. When he tried to rub up against her, she backed up. He followed her in her retreat until she had her back up against the picnic table. Crying out, the big cat reached up to claw at her thighs.

Cameron looked from where the cat was pitifully writhing in misery at her feet to the state police cruiser. There was no choice. The only way to get Irving home and cleaned up was to take him in the police car.

"You do realize that we're never going to live this down." She picked up the howling cat. Clinging to her with his front claws, he rubbed his face back and forth across her shoulder. "What happened? Did she get mad when she found out you were a cat in a skunk suit?"

❧ ❧ ❧ ❧

"What's that hideous smell?" Covering his nose with both hands, Donny stood in the bathroom doorway.

"Skunk," Cameron answered with a sigh of disgust.

Spying the open door, Irving clawed to get out of the bathtub where he was getting his second bath since Cameron had taken him to Joshua's house.

"Close the door before Irving gets out," she told Donny.

"I thought he was a cat that only looked like a skunk." He laughed after stepping inside and closing the door.

"Obviously, the skunk he had a run-in with at the park saw him for what he was and sprayed him."

Donny sniffed again. "Are you sure all that smell is Irving?" He moved in to catch a whiff of her hair. "I think that's you, too."

She dismissed his comment as a joke. "Cut it out."

The bathroom door opened, and Joshua stepped in with a cardboard box filled with tomato juice. "Lucky for you, the supermarket got a delivery today … and Chester is not known for its Bloody Marys." He handed a quart bottle to his son. "Open and start pouring."

"Into the tub?" Donny asked.

"Into the tub."

Standing over Cameron, who held Irving to prevent his escape, Donny poured the tomato juice into the tub. "Are you going to take a bath after Irving?"

Cameron laughed. "Why would I want to take a bath in tomato juice?"

Donny looked from her to Joshua, who was pouring a bottle of juice on her other side.

Following his gaze, she looked up at Joshua. "Stop it."

He bent over to sniff her hair and frowned.

"What?" she snapped.

Joshua reached into his pocket, took out his car keys, and handed them to Donny. "Go to the store to get another case of tomato juice."

Looking into the cat's eyes, which were filled with misery, she slumped. "Oh, Irving."

# Chapter Ten

Cameron wasn't a fan of heavy perfume. She preferred a light, soft scent of cologne. But the next morning, she felt as if her usual scent still held a skunk base, even though Joshua claimed it wasn't "that bad".

She suspected he was lying.

Anything was better than the smell of skunk. Even after a long soak in the tub of tomato juice, she couldn't get rid of the smell. It was impossible for her to get the shampoo to lather up enough to get it out of her hair.

*All this from just picking up Irving and riding home in the car with him?*

The next morning, she doused herself with a double dose of citrus-scented perfume that Sarah had left in her room before going off to the Naval Academy.

After two washings, her clothes, still smelling of skunk, got tossed into the garbage. Luckily, Joshua's younger daughter and Cameron were the same size. The clothes Sarah had left in her closet fit Cameron like they had been made for her.

Now that the detective could safely eliminate the mob as a suspect in killing Cheryl Smith, it was time to focus on her other suspects: friends and relatives of Angie Sullivan, which meant diving deeper into her disappearance and murder.

This being the case, Joshua had reason to ride along. Angie Sullivan's body had been found on the West Virginia side of the Ohio River. Until proven otherwise, they could assume she had been killed at the yacht club when her car was dumped into the river from their boat launch. That gave Joshua jurisdiction in the case.

It wasn't until Cameron and Joshua opened the doors to her police cruiser that they realized the skunk smell had permeated the interior.

Joshua jumped back and slammed the door shut. With his hand over his nose to block out the odor that felt like it had gone up his nose to attack his sinuses, he announced they were taking his car.

"What am I going to do?" Cameron's voice was high pitched.

"Take it to your motor pool and have them fumigate it."

"I can't do that."

She could envision the endless teasing that she was going to receive from the guys on the force. *I thought Irving was a cat. He is. Yeah. Right.*

Joshua was climbing into the driver's seat of his SUV. "Come on. I don't have all day. You can call your motor pool on your cell along the way and have them come pick it up."

She noticed that she had left her valise with all her case files in the back of the cruiser. She had been in such a rush to get Irving inside and bathed that she had forgotten to take her briefcase inside. "Maybe if I just leave the windows open for a few days."

"I don't think a few days will do it," Joshua said. "Put on your big girl pants, and get it fumigated." He rubbed the sides of his nose as if to eject the smell. His eyes were watering.

Holding her nose with one hand, Cameron threw open the door, grabbed the valise, slammed it shut, and then ran while taking in a deep breath of fresh, cold air.

Once they were inside Joshua's car, Cameron smiled softly when she saw Joshua wipe the tears from his eyes before starting the engine. "Imagine, as bad as we think this smell is, a cat's sense of smell is hundreds of times stronger than a human's. Think about it. Irving got a direct hit by that skunk. He's suffering a lot more than we are."

"I don't think so." He pointed over her shoulder to the living room bay window where they could see Irving tucked inside the curtains while sunning himself. They could make out his expression as being one of complete contentment.

"He wasn't that happy while he was getting his tomato juice bath," she said.

Joshua was holding the sides of his nose. "And I'm not the least bit happy now."

⁂

The alibi witness at the top of Cameron's list was Randy Vincent. He claimed that on the night Angie Sullivan had disappeared, he and Cheryl were hooking up in his van at the First Street Overlook in Chester.

Cameron studied her notes on Randy Vincent while Joshua drove along Locust Hill Road toward the countryside outside of Chester. "In the 1990's, Randy Vincent did five years in a prison in Pennsylvania for vehicular homicide—driving while under the influence."

"Sounds like my type of guy," he said with sarcasm. "Who'd he kill?"

"A thirty-two year old woman." She stopped to swallow. "Her four-month-old baby was in the car. Vincent came out without a scratch."

"I hate the guy already."

The report reminding her of another vehicular homicide case, Cameron closed the file. She couldn't read it anymore. "Maybe prison rehabilitated him."

As he turned the steering wheel to maneuver the SUV up a dirt country road leading back to the Vincent compound, Joshua glanced at her. He had seen that distant look in her eyes before.

When an awkward silence filled the car, Joshua wondered if she knew that he had learned through a background check about her short marriage, which she had yet to reveal to him.

Only four months after her wedding day, her husband, a Pennsylvania State trooper, was rundown by a drunk driver while he had another car pulled off to the side of the road for a routine traffic stop.

Cameron's silence about her husband made Joshua aware that he had no problem bringing up his late wife to her. He assumed it was because Valerie had been such a large part of his life. She had been the mother of his children.

Cameron's marriage had been brief, and they had no children. For her, it was less painful to pretend it had never happened, which could explain why she never mentioned it to him.

The dirt lane ended at a small farm hidden behind deep woods. Two horses, their coats caked with mud, grazed in a small field. The barn looked like it was only big enough for the two of them. The farmhouse was not much bigger.

After parking the SUV near the barn, Joshua and Cameron got out of the car. Before they could cross the driveway to the house, the front door opened and three big dogs bounded out toward them.

The woman at the door yelled over their barking. "They don't bite." She wasn't lying. Rather, they were more interested in taking the guests down by way of body slamming them to the ground.

Once they got a whiff of Cameron, the three dogs turned their attention to Joshua, who was able to remain on his feet while easing them to the ground.

"I guess they like you," she told him when they got to the door.

Joshua shot her a dirty look. "I don't think it's so much that they like me as they don't like skunk."

"Are you serious?" She glared at him until he gestured for her to follow the young woman, who had introduced herself as Mona, Vincent's daughter, inside the modest home.

They found Randy Vincent in the living room watching a talk show on a big screen television. The guests on the show, a man and woman, were screaming at each other while the audience and host egged them on.

According to the background check, Randy Vincent was a middle-aged man. However, he appeared to be living proof that it's not the years; it's the mileage. Stretched out on the well-worn sofa, he cradled the oxygen tank that rested in a sling under his arm. His stringy, greasy hair hung down to his neck. His goatee and mustache resembled a wire brush. He was wrapped up in a faded bathrobe that was as dirty as the filthy T-shirt and boxers, which he wore in lieu of pants. His face was yellow with jaundice.

He didn't break his stare when Mona showed them in and introduced them to her father. "Dad, this is the police detective I told you about who called last night," she yelled over the television before going back into the other room.

Joshua saw Mona watching them while busying herself at the kitchen counter.

Cameron stepped over to the sofa and held out her badge so that he could see it while introducing herself. "I'm investigating Cheryl Smith's and Angie Sullivan's murders.

Can I ask you a few questions?" When he didn't respond, she asked him if he understood what she was asking.

"I understood ya."

From where he was watching near the doorway, Joshua asked, "Can you turn down the volume so we can talk?"

With a glare in Joshua's direction, Randy held up the remote, pointed it at the television, and blasted the volume.

Cameron and Joshua exchanged glances. She took the lead. "Mr. Vincent, if you don't want to talk to us here, I can take you into the police station to talk."

"Shut up, bitch," he replied in a loud voice.

"What did you call her?" Joshua crossed the room toward him so quickly that the man on the sofa rose as if he were ready to take him on.

Cameron's arm shot out to catch Joshua in the chest to stop him. "I'll handle this."

"I know my rights." Randy eased back down onto the sofa. "I don't have to talk to either of you."

"We're trying to find out who killed Cheryl Smith," she replied.

With a curse, Randy gathered up his oxygen tank and pulled himself up from off the sofa.

"Don't you want to know who killed her?" she asked.

Tucking the tank under his arm like a football, he shuffled down the hallway toward the back of the house while extracting a cigarette from a pack.

"She was supposed to be your friend," she called after him.

When he opened the door in the hallway, the odor of stale cigarette smoke shot out. He shot her a hate-filled glare over his shoulder before going inside and slamming the door.

Cameron looked over at Joshua. "That went well."

"He's right." Joshua led her back to the kitchen and to the door. "He doesn't have to talk to you."

"I'm sorry for my father," Mona apologized as she led them to the front door. "He's an A-Number-One jerk. The only reason I put up with him is because I know if I didn't, he'd be on the streets."

"You're a good daughter," Joshua told her.

"No, I'm not," she replied. "I'm an enabler. Maybe if he was out on the streets he'd straighten up."

"Then he'd be my problem," Joshua said.

"Which is why I enable him, to protect society." She followed them out onto the porch. "I'll walk you to your car."

Cameron and Joshua exchanged questioning expressions while dodging moving dogs on their way down the steps. The canines seemed intent on tripping them.

At the bottom of the porch steps, Mona whispered, "Cheryl Smith didn't kill Angie Sullivan."

Cameron stopped.

Joshua turned around to face Mona. A hard life of caring for her father made her appear older than her actual years. Even so, Angie Sullivan's disappearance was before her time. "And you know that how?"

"He told me." She tossed her head to indicate the man inside the house who was smoking a cigarette while cradling his oxygen tank. "He told me everything when it hit the news about finding Cherry Pickens in Hookstown." She scoffed. "He's so proud of himself having screwed sex symbol Cherry Pickens. I had no idea who she was, until I remembered that he has a box of those smut tapes in his room, and he watches them at night after a six pack of beer. I recognized her picture in the newspaper from those tapes."

Crooking her finger at them, she led them across the driveway to move away from the house where he might hear. "He told me about how the police thought Cherry, Cheryl, had killed Angie Sullivan, this girl she had a big fight with at the skating rink in Hookstown."

"But he made a statement to the police that she didn't do it," Cameron said. "He was Cheryl's alibi."

Mona confirmed that she was right with a nod of her head. "They were having sex in the back of his van."

"Was he telling the truth?" Joshua asked.

"I have no doubt that he was telling me the truth," she said. "He told me the rest of the story—what he didn't tell the police and didn't want to tell you."

"He wasn't with her all night?" Cameron asked.

"He was drunk and high," Mona said. "After they had sex, he passed out and didn't wake up until after the sun had risen the next morning."

"Then he can't alibi her," the detective said.

Mona grinned. "But he knows she didn't do it."

"How can he be so sure if he was passed out?" Joshua asked.

"Because she told him." When Joshua and Cameron exchanged doubtful glances, she added, "She also told him that she knew who did kill Angie Sullivan."

"And he believed her?" Cameron scoffed.

"He had proof."

Cameron squinted at her. "What type of proof?"

"Not actual evidence." Mona glanced over her shoulder. They could see that she wanted to make sure her father wasn't watching her betray the secret he wanted kept because of his own nastiness. "Dad told me that the night that Cheryl had gotten into that fight with Angie, she was bitching to him about how she had no money. When they went to the First Street overlook, while they were drinking and smoking, she told him that she had figured it out. She would have to work over a year for that fast food joint where she flipped burgers, and not spend any money on anything, before she could save enough money to go to Hollywood. That was her dream, to go to Hollywood and be in the movies."

"Which she did," Cameron said.

"After Angie went missing and the police started asking around," Mona said, "Dad knew that he was so out of it that Cheryl could have left the van and done something stupid like hunt down and kill Angie." She lowered her voice. "Dad said that Cheryl had one nasty temper. So he went and asked her flat out if she had killed Angie. She laughed at him and said that she didn't, but she knew who did. He asked her how, but she refused to tell him anything about it. She said it was so good that she was keeping it to herself."

Mona cocked her head at them. "Dad didn't believe her, but she was his friend, so he backed her up and alibied her. Then, ten days later, lo and behold, Cheryl was on her way to Hollywood. When she went to see Dad to tell him goodbye and thank him for alibiing her, he asked her where she got the money. She laughed at him and said that she had a benefactor who was paying her way to Hollywood in style." She nodded her head. "That was when he believed her that she knew who did it."

"But if she knew who killed Angie Sullivan, why didn't she tell the police when they accused her of doing it?" Cameron asked.

With a distant look in his eyes, Joshua muttered, "Because she wanted to go to Hollywood and needed someone to pay her way. It was more beneficial to her to keep her mouth shut and blackmail the real killer."

"I'm only telling you what Dad told me he knew," Mona said. "I hope it helps you."

Joshua shook her hand. "You've been a big help. Thank you so much." He was in the car before Cameron had time to finish shaking her hand. "Get in the car, Cam. I have something to show you."

She had barely fastened her seat belt before Joshua was tearing down the lane to Locust Hill Road. "Where are we going in such a hurry?"

"Someplace quiet to neck."

❧ ❧ ❧ ❧

The First Street Overlook in Chester had once been the home of the Chester Bridge, referred to now as the Old Chester Bridge. After the bridge had been torn down in the 1960's, the entrance way that had led onto the bridge was converted into an overlook. With a fantastic view of the river, residents could sit on benches and enjoy the view and fresh air while having lunch. In the evening, couples would park and kiss. They didn't so much anymore.

Over the years, rowdy, young people had driven the quiet lovers out. After the vandalism of a plaque honoring Dr. Russ Pugh, a late town doctor who had been a mentor of Tad; Joshua had surveillance cameras installed in hopes of catching the culprits. So far, there hadn't been any luck.

"This is gorgeous," Cameron said in a breathy voice when she saw the expansive view up and down the river.

From where Joshua had parked the SUV up at the railing, she had a clear view of East Liverpool across the river. On her left, she could see all the way down past the Newell Bridge. To the right, she could see the houses along the river bank all the way down to the new Chester Bridge. "I can imagine what this is like at night … with all the lights across the river …"

"It's one of the best views in town," he told her.

She turned to him.

He had that soft look in his blue eyes. The corner of his mouth curled. When she leaned toward him, he cupped his hand behind her head and brought her in closer to taste her lips. When he started to pull away, she grasped his face to bring him back to kiss him again and again.

With a smile, he wrapped his arms around her. "We should have come here sooner." She was reaching inside his coat when he remembered the surveillance cameras he had installed to curtail vandalism. With visions of Hancock County Sheriff Curt Sawyer having a good chuckle while watching him and Cameron smooching at the First Street Overlook, he pushed her hands away.

"Later," he said. "That's not what I wanted to show you." He threw open the car door. With a sense of relief, the cold, fresh air cooled his passion.

When she met him around at the front of the car, he led her by the hand up to the railing where the view of the shoreline stretched up and down the river.

"What?" She tried to keep the whine out of her voice from his abrupt end to their romantic connection.

He was peering over the railing and down the river toward the Newell Bridge. "Mona said that her father stated that he and Cheryl were making out in the back of his van right here at the overlook."

"That's also what he stated in his alibi for her." Thinking that she should have come to investigate the scene in person earlier, Cameron nodded. "He claimed they were in the van all night. But now we know he was inebriated and passed out, so she could have left."

"Obviously, she did." Joshua leaned against the railing and folded his arms. "How else would she know who really killed Angie?"

She gazed at him. A gust of winter wind blew their hair across their faces. She tossed her head to get the locks tickling her cheeks off her face.

Joshua guided her by her shoulders up to the rail. Standing behind her, he wrapped his arms around her and kissed her on the back of her neck. The warmth of his body cut the chill from the wind whipping around them on the overlook.

She followed the aim of his finger to look in the direction of the Newell Bridge and down to the shoreline. Less than a mile away, there was a café and docks that had been shut down for the winter season.

"It's the yacht club." She felt his hot breath in her ear. "The same yacht club where Angie's car and body were found." The events came crashing together in her mind. "After Randy passed out in the van, Cheryl came out to look at the view."

"Or maybe she heard Angie fighting her killer," Joshua said.

"Whatever the case, she saw the murder and the killer from here." When she turned to him, their eyes met. "That means the motive for Cheryl's murder was blackmail. She came running back here to blackmail the killer again to help her escape from the mob."

"Exactly," Joshua said. "We find Angie's killer, and we'll find Cheryl's killer."

Cameron's cell phone vibrated in her pocket. She had to pull away from him to take it out of its case where it was clipped to her belt.

Without her to warm him up, Joshua stuffed his hands in his pockets and shivered while she read her text message.

"Not so fast, cowboy," she told him while reading the message.

"What is it?"

She held up the cell phone for him to read. "Forensics managed to pull up prints from the inside of that ice box. They belong to Doris Sullivan, Angie's sister-slash-mother."

# Chapter Eleven

"Are you kidding me?" Joshua replied to her news about forensics lifting Doris Sullivan's fingerprints from the freezer.

"They were inside," Cameron explained. "They also found traces of molasses and oats."

"Doris raises Thoroughbreds." He followed her back to the car. "What about the serial number?" He unlatched the passenger door and held it open for her. "Were they able to trace that back to her?"

Before sliding into her seat, Cameron paused to shake her head in response to his question. "The manufacturer's records don't go that far back. But they were able to tell us that model was built back in the early fifties."

"No wonder it didn't work." After closing her door, he went around to slide into the driver's seat and fastened his seat belt.

"Cheryl could have been hidden in that freezer somewhere else, and then transported to Albert's place when the killer found out what a hoarder he was. He—*or she*—thought, or rather hoped, no one would ever discover it." She pointed to the road for him to turn around. "Our next stop is the Sullivan Farm."

Joshua shook his head. "Our next stop is the church."

"Why? Are we late for a funeral?"

"No," he laughed. "It's Wednesday afternoon. Doris Sullivan and the ladies meet at the church for their afternoon Bible study. If we want to question Doris about that freezer, we need to go to the church."

"Now there's something I've never done," she replied, "interview a murder suspect in a church."

"You may get to do more than interview a suspect." Joshua pulled his car into the parking lot behind the church. He pointed across the lot to a royal blue Cadillac parked next to the space reserved for the church pastor. "Mildred Hildebrand is here. Would you believe that woman has been driving blue caddies since before I was born? When you're in Chester and you see a blue caddie, you know it belongs to Mildred Hildebrand." He then pointed at a black dual-wheeled pickup truck parked on the other side of his SUV. "Doris Sullivan was driving pickups before it was chic for women to drive trucks."

Recalling the tension she had witnessed between the two elderly women during the clean-up at Albert's house, Cameron said, "This should be fun."

~ ~ ~ ~

Cameron and Joshua could hear the cat fight from the moment they walked through the church doors. Instinctively, she put her hand on her gun. Joshua reached out to stop her and shook his head. When she looked at him questioningly, a grin crossed his face. Before he could explain, an elderly woman came running into the sanctuary from the back meeting rooms.

"Oh, Joshua, I'm so glad you're here." She pointed in the direction of the shrieks. "They're at it again."

They followed her to a Sunday school classroom in the back of the church. There, they found Doris Sullivan and Mildred Hildebrand rolling on the floor and pulling each other's gray hair while four bewildered-looking women stood over them. Doris and Mildred were shrieking like alley cats fighting over a single bite of tuna.

Dressed in a purple dress and a red bonnet, one of the class members was clapping her hands in a vain attempt to get their attention. "Ladies! Ladies! Stop this right now!"

Joshua grabbed Mildred around her thick waist and pulled her to her feet from where she straddled Doris.

"Tramp!" Mildred yelled. "You're nothing but a damned cheap, jealous slut!"

"And you're a stuck-up old biddie!" Doris leaped to her feet with the agility of a teenager.

"I'm a great-grandmother! How dare you talk to me like that!"

"Ladies!" the red-hatted woman snapped in a loud voice. "I won't have cursing in God's house! I won't have it!"

"Why do you even come here?" Mildred yelled. "You don't know the first thing about Christian charity. Your own sister hated you!"

"How dare you!" Doris shoved her in her plump chest.

Mildred fell back against Joshua. The unexpected force of her body against his knocked the two of them off their feet and down to the floor in the corner of the small room.

Cameron tried to pull the enraged woman off them, but before she could do so Doris yanked off her opponent's wig to reveal a head of thin, gray strands of hair. Unaware that she was still sitting on top of Joshua, Mildred attempted to cover her head while screaming as loud as her lungs would allow.

The other women, long aware of Mildred's wig, covered their mouths to hide their amusement. Stunned, Cameron's mouth dropped open. Shrieking with delight, Doris ran out of the room while triumphantly waving the hair piece.

"You spiteful little bitch!" Mildred scrambled off of Joshua and gave chase.

"I don't believe this," one of the women muttered.

Cameron helped Joshua struggle to his feet, and the two of them ran out into the sanctuary where they found Doris skipping through one row of pews before turning to dance along the next one.

"This proves you're a phony, Millie!"

When Mildred tried to reach for the wig, Doris jumped up onto the seat to hold it out of her reach. "You never have forgiven me for stealing Ralph from you!"

"You didn't steal him!" Doris claimed. "I left him!"

Mildred scoffed. "Who do you think you're kidding? Your family had to send you away to boarding school to get you to leave him alone!"

Watching Mildred over her shoulder, Doris ran down the center aisle towards the main doors where her getaway was cut off by Joshua who caught her in his arms.

"That's enough," he said.

"She started it!" Tears pouring from her eyes, Mildred pointed an accusing finger at her adversary. "She's been spreading despicable rumors about Ralph."

"Liar!" Doris lunged for her, but Joshua yanked her back.

"Stop it!" His commanding voice bounced off the walls and ceilings of the church to capture everyone's attention. "Stop it, right now!" He grabbed the wig. "Have you forgotten where you are?! You're behaving like a couple of heathens!"

The reminder made the two women look guiltily at their feet.

Joshua handed the wig to Mildred. "Go put your hair on, and clean yourself up."

Tears in her eyes, Mildred hurried down the stairs to the ladies' bathroom.

Joshua turned his attention to Doris, who was still looking at her feet like a naughty child. "Doris Sullivan, if I catch you stirring up trouble again, I'm telling the pastor, and you'll be removed for any position of leadership. Got it?" He clapped his hands to capture everyone's attention. "Break it up. The show's over."

While he ushered the women back to the Sunday school classroom, Joshua caught Cameron's eye. No words were necessary to communicate the next step in their investigation. She turned heel to head to the ladies room to help Mildred get a few things off her abundant chest.

❧ ❧ ❧ ❧

Downstairs, Mildred Hildebrand was still sputtering with fury. She was so enraged that she failed to notice that she had put her wig on crooked. Since she was considered a church leader, she felt obligated to defend her role in the scene that the police detective had witnessed.

"She's crazy," Mildred raged with tears in her eyes. "You see that, don't you? No sane person would have said those things to another woman." She choked. "I'm so upset that I've had to call my daughter to come take me home." She held out her hand for Cameron to see it shaking. "Look at what that woman did to me. I'm shaking like a leaf."

While she listened to her with sympathy, Cameron made a concerted effort not to stare at the clownishly crooked hair piece. She wet a paper towel and offered it to Mildred for her to wash her face.

"She always has been crazy with jealously of me." Mildred wiped the tears from her eyes, blew her nose, and held up her head to regain her dignity. "She used to make like she was high and mighty because she went to boarding school overseas, but I know the truth. Her own sister hated Doris because she was always picking on her. That's because she was jealous of Angie, too. Doris was always jealous of pretty girls. Those two fought like cats and dogs."

"Have you two always been rivals?" Cameron asked.

"No," Mildred choked. "Would you believe we used to be best friends? The very best of friends. Of course, I was the pretty one." She struck a dancing pose. "I was also quite a dancer. Doris was the tomboy. On Saturday afternoons, I would go to her farm, and we would spend the whole afternoon riding. And then on Saturday night, we would go to the Silver Slipper."

The detective's blank expression caused Mildred to scoff. "The Silver Slipper. Surely, you've heard of it." Sighing with regret, she turned around to peer into the mirror. "I guess that was before your time."

"What was the Silver Slipper?" Cameron asked her reflection.

"It was the dance hall in Hookstown. The American Legion is there now—at the end of the Silver Slipper Road."

"Which runs off of Snowden Road," the detective noted.

"Exactly," Mildred said. "When the Silver Slipper closed, they opened a skating rink across the street, and the young people started going there. The Melody Lane Skating Rink was where all of my daughters' met their husbands. It burnt down I don't know how many years ago."

Cameron noted, "The Melody Lane was where Angie Sullivan was last seen alive."

"Yes, it was. My daughter Gail was there that night. She saw the whole awful thing." With another sigh, she straightened her wig. "Young people knew how to behave back in my day. We went to the Silver Slipper to dance, not brawl, and no one danced better than me. That was where Doris and I met Ralph. Of course, we both fell head over heels."

A look of determination crossed Mildred's face. "But he *chose me*, probably because he could see what a spiteful little bitch Doris really is. She never forgave me for it—even after over fifty years."

"Mom, what have you done now?" With a sigh that could only be described as maternal, deep and tired, Gail Hildebrand came into the ladies' rest room. She held the door open with one arm, and the other hand on her wide hip. An expression of amusement and disgust filled her face. "When are you going to learn to turn the other cheek when it comes to Doris Sullivan?"

"She started it," Mildred whirled around to announce. "She was saying that your father left me. I couldn't let her get away with saying things like that about my husband." She folded her arms under her plump breasts. "But then, what do you know about standing by your man?"

The sound of the women speaking drifted down the stairs. The determined look hardened and Mildred charged out of the room.

"Mom," Gail called after her, "I thought you wanted me to take you home."

"I can't leave my group." She was up the stairs as fast as her plump legs could carry her.

Gail raised an eyebrow in Cameron's direction and smiled. "We can't risk Doris Sullivan taking control of the Bible study group."

"I guess you've been on the sidelines to witness this feud between your mother and Doris from almost the beginning."

"Oh, yeah." Gail rolled her eyes. "You learn how you don't want to be when you grow up. And what to marry … and divorce."

"The stand by your man crack," Cameron noted.

"My husband had to stray once, and I kicked him to the curb. Mom never forgave me for that. She claims my love was conditional, and that I'm an unforgiving woman. Hey, I forgave him … but I still kicked him to the curb."

Cameron recalled seeing her and Ned Carter's furtive glances while they were talking at the casino, and him hiding her in his office while she questioned him.

"You can forgive someone without being a fool," Gail claimed. "There was no way I was going to put up with what Mom has had to put up with from my father. She honestly believes no one knows about it."

"How about you playing the other woman cheating with the married man?"

Gail's eyes narrowed. She caught her breath. "I have no idea what you mean." Her voice had gone up a full octave.

"If your friendship with Ned Carter is so innocent, why did you feel the need to hide when I went to interview him?"

Gail's cheeks turned pink. After a few attempts to explain, in which she sputtered out indistinguishable noises, she finally said, "We didn't mean to fall in love."

"Does Brianne know?"

Her face went from pink to white. "No!" As if her knees had grown too weak to hold her, she lowered herself into one of two chairs placed in the rest room for nursing mothers. "You have no idea what a temper Brianne has."

"I thought Cheryl Smith was the one with a temper."

Gail chuckled. "Cheryl Smith's temper was public. Brianne unleashes her temper behind closed doors. Only those close to her have seen it."

Finding this revelation enlightening, Camera sat down in the other chair. "Have you seen it?"

"Thankfully, no, but I know others who have. Ned has seen it many times. When something happens to upset her, she's all smiles and graciousness in public. Then, as soon as the door closes, lamps are flying and people are running for cover."

"Wow." The detective urged her to continue.

"That's if you're lucky," Gail said. "If you're not lucky, Brianne will go behind your back and connive and manipulate something far worse."

"Like what?"

Gail's eyes met hers.

The two women stared at each other. Cameron felt as if she were reading what she wanted to tell her telepathically. "What did she do to Angie Sullivan?"

"Angie?"

"Doris Sullivan's sister," Cameron explained.

"How good of a detective are you?"

Cameron noticed that Gail's hair was also strawberry-blond and her eyes blue. *I wonder ...* "How good do you think I am?"

Gail lowered her voice to a stage whisper. "Good enough to know that Angie was my half-sister." As Cameron sat up in her chair, she added, "That's something else Mom is in denial about."

"How did you feel about that?"

"Angie was my friend." She swallowed a catch in her throat. "I loved her like a sister." She lowered her eyes to her hands. "She died not knowing we were sisters."

Cameron's low voice matched hers. "But you knew."

"It was my twelfth birthday party at our house. Angie was fourteen. I had invited her to it because she was my friend from here at church. We had all gone outside to cut the cake, and I came into the kitchen to get something. I overheard Dad and Doris talking in the dining room. Doris said that Angie was wanting to know who her father was, and she wanted to tell her. Dad was furious because he said Mom would be devastated if she found out the truth about Angie."

"Does your mother buy the story about Angie being Doris' sister?"

Gail smirked. "She has to. Dad was dating both of them until Mom rammed him into marrying her. If she admitted to herself that Angie was Doris' daughter, she'd have to face that her husband was the father. Mom would rather kill herself than face the fact that her husband has been with anyone besides her." She added with a nervous laugh, "Worse, that people knew about it. The Queen of the Church Ladies' husband fathering another woman's baby—now there's a scandal for you."

The detective said, "Wasn't this family secret the topic of the fight that night that Angie disappeared?"

"So you know about that," she said, "but I bet you don't know the whole story behind it."

"Enlighten me."

"In their senior year, someone beat out Brianne for prom queen."

"And that was—"

"Angie," Gail said. "Now I went to Oak Glen High School. They all went to South Side High School. But I went to the rink and all of us mixed together there. Back then, Ned hardly noticed me. I was chubby—"

"Get to Brianne's conniving and manipulation involving Angie."

"Brianne and Angie were best friends," she explained. "Angie had done what best friends do. She confided to Brianne about Doris being her mother. So, Brianne was armed with this weapon. Plus, she had two other things going for her; looks and money. She knew how truly nasty Cheryl Smith was. So Brianne proceeded to seduce Cheryl's boyfriend away from her. Ned was sneaking around with Brianne, who he couldn't resist. Cheryl knew he was sneaking around. So Brianne told her that it was Angie. Then, she gave Cheryl the ammunition to truly wound her—all because Angie beat her out for prom queen." Gail scoffed. "Of course, at the prom, she pretended it didn't matter; but behind the scenes ..."

"She buried Angie by spilling the family secret to reveal to all," Cameron said, "while making Cheryl look like the chief bad guy. How clever."

"Everyone knew about it."

"Except your mother," the detective said in a low voice.

"She knows," Gail said. "She only pretends she doesn't."

"She's not the only one." Cameron looked at Gail. Here's a woman not cut out to be the other woman. Ned was too good looking to expect him to cheat on a looker like Brianne with someone so down to earth. "What do you think Brianne would do if she were to find out about Ned cheating on her with you?"

Gail's face turned red.

"What does Brianne have on him? Did Ned see Cheryl Smith when she came back?"

"No," Gail blurted out.

"Do you know that for certain?"

"Yes, Ned wouldn't lie to me." When Cameron grinned at her patronizingly, Gail said, "*Ned* was the one who requested the audit ... the audit that everyone is talking about. Someone has been skimming money out of the Mountaineer's accounts. The deeper we dug, the more it looked like Ned. He requested the audit to find out who has been trying to frame him. I wouldn't be surprised if it was Brianne because she knows about us."

"That's what Ned tells you."

"That's what I know," Gail said. "We can prove it. Someone is hacking into the accounting programs, using Ned's login and manipulating the numbers to skim money from the resort. He changed his login. Less than a day later, they had hacked in under his new login."

"Have you had a computer forensics team in to trace the hacker?"

Gail nodded. "The state prosecutor's office sent a team up." She lowered her voice. "We're keeping it hush-hush because we don't want to clue in whoever it is that's doing it."

Cameron found it difficult to believe Ned was as innocent as Gail was claiming. She didn't know if it was because of his good looks and past, or because of Gail's starry-eyed gaze when she talked about him.

"One of those weekends that the hacker broke into the account was last Valentine's Day weekend." The pink in Gail's cheeks deepened. "Brianne had told Ned that she had to go away to a conference and would be working all weekend. Ned and I used the opportunity to go to the Clay-Byrn Castle Lodge in Ohio for a romantic getaway. While we were gone, someone transferred twenty-five thousand dollars from the resort under Ned's account."

"If it was an online transfer, Ned could have done it from his phone."

Gail was shaking her head. "There's no internet at the Clay-Byrn Castle. They have none on purpose. No television. No cell phone service. No phones in the rooms. It's an escape. Ned and I were there the whole weekend. He couldn't have sent an e-mail if his life depended on it." She concluded her case with, "I think Brianne knows about us, and she's framing him. And of course, if they do decide Ned did it, once our affair comes out, I'll be going down along with him."

"Seriously?" Doris reacted to Joshua's question about the freezer with a laugh that reminded him of the Wicked Witch of the West in *The Wizard of Oz*. "It was *my* freezer that Cheryl Smith was found in?" She squinted at him. "Everyone said when you took up with that lady cop that you had lost your mind."

Her surprise turned to insult. "Look, I gave them permission to dig up Angie's body so that they could look for proof that Cheryl killed her. Now, you're accusing me of killing that slut that killed my baby!" She laughed again. "If I did kill Cheryl, don't you think I'd admit to it? I challenge any jury to convict me for doing the world a favor."

Joshua looked around the sanctuary where he had taken her to discuss the matter away from the other women in the study group. His effort to not embarrass her was in vain. While he lowered his voice, she raised hers. "Tell me about when you went down into the basement at Albert Gordon's house."

"Are we really going to go over that again?" Doris looked past him to the altar.

"Maybe now that you've had more time to think about it, you can remember what you saw."

Doris shook her head. "I saw a lot. Albert's cellar was a mess. There was stuff everywhere. I could have found a bomb making kit right in front of me, and I would never have noticed it because of all the junk."

Joshua folded his arms and leaned over toward where the old woman was sitting at the other side of the pew. "How did you feel about him representing Cheryl Smith in that hearing where the judge decided the police couldn't keep her from going to Hollywood?"

"I was extremely hurt," she said. "But he apologized and explained why he did it."

"Which was?"

"Innocent until proven guilty." She shrugged her thin shoulders. "I eventually forgave him."

"Did you know before Albert's death that he was a hoarder?"

"No," she replied. "After his wife died, Albert shut me out along with everyone else."

"You two were neighbors and friends," the lawyer noted. "You have both grown up on the same road. Your farms are next to each other. He let you use his fields after he let go of his livestock. You had to notice that something was happening."

"Yes," Doris snapped. "I noticed that his wife died, and he wanted to be left alone. I felt the same way when Angie disappeared. I understood. So I left him alone … I left him alone to wallow in his own junk. Is there anything wrong with that?"

"Unless you decided to take advantage of it and slip a dead body into his basement to hide it." He asked, "Do you by any chance have a key to his farmhouse?"

She jumped up to her feet. "I think it's time for me to go."

"I'll take that as a yes," he replied.

"I'm an old farm girl," Doris said in a gruff voice.

Joshua waited in silence.

"Why on God's green earth would I want to kill some Hollywood porn star and stuff her body in an old, broken down freezer?"

"Because you blamed her for killing Angie," he said in a whisper. "Fingerprints don't lie."

"Maybe I put them there years ago," she suggested.

"Yes, you did," he replied. "Like when you stuffed Cheryl Smith's body in the freezer after killing her."

She lowered her voice to a growl. "I meant when I used to own that freezer. Maybe it was an old one that I had sold back before Cheryl Smith came running back to town, and whomever I sold it to killed her instead."

The suggestion that her fingerprints had remained in the freezer long after she had gotten rid of it was a stretch, but Joshua played along. "Do you remember having an old freezer that you sold to a possible suspect?"

After a long pause, her lips curled. "Yes, I do remember one." The glare came back to her eyes. Her mouth grew tight. "I don't remember what year it was … it was after they had found Angie. I know that. I donated an old freezer just like the one you described to the church yard sale."

"Do you remember who bought—"

"Mildred Hildebrand."

Joshua sighed.

"How could I forget? That witch then turned around and sued me. Sued me!" A grin came to her face when she recalled, "The judge tossed the case out of court, of course; but still, I had to go down there all because that petty—"

"It was a piece of junk!" Mildred came galloping into the sanctuary from the hallway.

"It was a donation to a yard sale," Doris said.

"It broke after only five days."

"You only paid fifty dollars for it. What did you expect?"

When the two women charged at each other, Joshua stood up between them and held out his arms to keep them apart. "What did I say about you two starting trouble?"

His warning was enough to make them back up and fall silent.

"Very good." He turned to Mildred. "What happened to the freezer you bought at the yard sale?"

She scoffed. "What do you think happened? It wouldn't work. So I had Ralph haul it out to the landfill."

He took a chance and asked, "I don't suppose you remember what year that was?"

Mildred made a noise from deep in her throat. "Of course, I do. I have a memory like an elephant."

Doris scoffed.

Mildred folded her hands across her midriff. "I remember everything based on what was happening with my family at the time. I bought that freezer at the yard sale—I'll have you know that I don't usually buy used items. I also make it a point not to buy wholesale or at discount stores, but the yard sale that year was to raise money for underprivileged families in—"

"Today, Mrs. Hildebrand!" Joshua blurted out.

"May 1985."

Surprised that she was able to narrow it down to the month, he asked, "How can you be so sure?"

Pleased by his reaction, Mildred stuck out her chest. She smirked when she answered, "It was the same month Trish, my third daughter, graduated from high school. She was with me that day when we bought it."

# Chapter Twelve

Their luncheon date turned into a massage session in Joshua's study.

That morning, Joshua was quietly reading *The Review* while sipping his coffee when he heard the garbage truck turn the corner. That was when he discovered Donny had failed to take the garbage cans out to the curb. Wearing only his bathrobe and slippers, Joshua slid down the icy driveway in a race against the garbage collectors to get the cans out to the curb before they drove by.

Joshua won by a nose. He also lost when, on his way inside, he slipped on the ice and landed flat on his back in the driveway.

After listening to him groaning through half of lunch, Cameron ordered him to take off his shirt and lie down on the rug. Intrigued with what she was going to do, he complied. Once he was on his stomach, she straddled his back.

"We have an audience," he told her.

Her hands on his shoulders, Cameron stopped to see Irving sitting in the doorway. His glaring eyes were aimed at Joshua, who was staring back at him. "Irving," she said in a sharp tone. "Behave."

The black and white cat paused as if to consider her order before standing up, his tail straight up in the air, and stalking across the study to Joshua's desk. There, he waited.

Suspicious, Joshua twisted around to see what he had in mind.

Once Irving was assured he had Joshua's attention, he jumped up onto the desk, circled around on top of his papers, and plopped down.

"He did that on purpose," Joshua said.

"Ignore him." Cameron urged him back down.

"Easy for you to say. He doesn't hate you."

"Put Irving out of your mind, and concentrate on my hands." She resumed giving his back a deep massage.

Within seconds of pushing her attitude-filled skunk cat out of his mind, Joshua replaced his groans with moans of pleasure. "Where did you learn to do this?"

"My late husband used to come home with horrible backaches from riding in the cruiser all day. One of my massages would snap him right back into shape."

An awkward silence filled the room. It was the first time Cameron had ever mentioned her late husband.

Joshua tried to remain cool. *Bingo! She knows that I know about him.*

Her soft slender hands felt so warm on his back that Joshua feared he was going to fall asleep.

Her voice woke him up. "Harry called me a bitch."

"Detective Shannon," Joshua recalled the retired detective who had first worked Angie Sullivan's disappearance. "What did you do to him?"

"Why do you think I did something to him?"

"He wouldn't call you that if you didn't give him a reason."

"I called to tell him about uncovering the rumor, which proved to be true, about Doris being Angie's mother," she said. "Even if Brianne, Ned, and Kyle kept quiet; Harry should have found out about it during his investigation from someone or somewhere. He says he did hear murmurings, but claimed it was nothing more than schoolgirl gossip mongering and irrelevant. I told him that until it was proven to not be part of the case it has to be treated as a lead, and he should have put it in his notes." She clutched his shoulders with her hands so hard, her fingernails dug into his flesh. "That was when he called me a bitch."

Saying nothing, Joshua rubbed his face into the carpet.

"Aren't you going to say anything?" She wanted confirmation that she was right, and Detective Shannon was guilty of mishandling his investigation.

Instead, he asked, "What do you want me to say?"

"You always have something to say. It's who you are."

He sighed. "You're both right."

"You are *such* a politician."

"I am *not* a politician."

"Yes, you are." With a laugh in her voice, she halted the massage with her hands on his shoulders. "Don't tell me you don't have an opinion about this. Harry should have reported what Cheryl and Angie were fighting about that night. It could have led to the motive for her murder. How could he not have known that? And I don't understand how you can't see that."

After a long heavy sigh, Joshua said, "It's a double-edge sword."

"What are you talking about?"

"You're not in Philadelphia anymore, Cam." With a pain-filled groan, he twisted to tell her over his shoulder, "Doris Sullivan is a farmer in Hookstown. In these parts, a word of gossip flies as swiftly as the winter wind off the river, and it cuts even deeper. Maybe it's the downside of everyone knowing and caring about their neighbor. Some people don't know where to draw the line between needing to know out of genuine concern and wanting to know in order to cast judgment."

Cameron said, "I'm not casting judgment. I'm trying to find out who killed Cheryl Smith. Don't forget that Angie Sullivan's murder is your case. You have a genuine interest in this family secret that could prove to be a motive for her murder."

"I'm very aware of that," he said. "But Angie was the only family Doris had left, and she lost her. Why hurt her any further by publicizing a family secret that may or may not be true, and which may or may not be relevant to Angie's murder?"

"There's a big, thick line between publicizing gossip and investigating a lead," she said. "Besides, Gail Hildebrand told me flat-out that it's not a rumor. It's true. She overheard her father and Doris talking about it."

"Ralph?"

"Yes, Ralph. Ralph Hildebrand was Angie's father."

"I'll be—" He stopped. "Ralph knew?"

She nodded her head. "According to his daughter Gail."

"How about Mildred?"

"Gail says she's in denial."

"La-la Land." He felt her shift her weight to concentrate on his middle back. In doing so, she pressed the air out of his lungs. "Mildred confirmed that she had bought Doris' freezer … and hauled it out to the landfill. That means it was out of Doris' possession when Cheryl came back to town." He turned his head. She was so close that he could see the green specks in her hazel eyes. "*Ralph* took it to the landfill."

"Ralph was Angie's birth father." She rose to allow him to sit up. "Doris Sullivan was also the only one who went down into that basement that morning."

Joshua shook his head. "Other people had been in the basement."

"Moments before I noticed the bomb?" she asked. "Doris Sullivan lives next door. She's known Albert their whole lives."

"Albert also played a big role in Cheryl leaving town after Angie's disappearance," Joshua pointed out. "Doris says she forgave him but, being a parent, I find it hard to believe she would have been able to completely let it go. I know I'd have a hard time forgiving someone for that."

"At some point over the years, Albert had to have given her a key to his place for in case of an emergency ..." she said, "or hiding a dead body."

He took her hand, placed it on his bare shoulder, and turned around to stretch out on the floor. The unspoken message was for her to return to work at massaging his back while thinking about that. "Even if that was Doris' freezer, it was out of her possession at the time of Cheryl's murder. Cheryl knew that she was a person of interest in Angie's murder. Doris Sullivan would have been the last person she would have gone to for help when she came back to town."

"Unless Doris killed Angie." She reminded him, "According to Randy's daughter, Cheryl saw the murder, and the killer paid her way to Hollywood. Otherwise, where did she get the money to leave town back in 1978?"

"I don't think Doris killed Angie," he said. "I can see her killing Cheryl, but not Angie."

"Maybe Ralph killed Angie to keep word from getting out about him being her father. Mildred is an extremely proud woman," she said. "Appearances are most important to her. I've seen more than one murder where the wife flipped out after finding out that her husband had a child by another woman. Knowing that, Ralph may have felt like he had no choice but to get rid of Angie when Cheryl started spreading the word about her being Doris' daughter and not her sister." She tapped his shoulder with her fingertip. "Ralph Hildebrand certainly had the dough to pay Cheryl's way to

Hollywood. Not only that, but he was the last one in possession of the freezer. When Cheryl came back for more dough, he killed her to put an end to the blackmail." In delight, she patted his back with both hands. "There you have it. We've solved both murders."

With a shake of his head, Joshua rolled over onto his back. "Killing Angie wouldn't have achieved that motive. If anything, it started tongues wagging more about her."

"You're thinking like a well-adjusted person," she said. "With Angie out of the picture, Mildred was better able to ignore the truth."

"How is it possible that a looker like Cherry Pickens comes flying into a small town like Chester or Hookstown in a fire-engine red Ferrari and nobody notice?" he wondered out loud. "What happened to that car?"

Without his asking, she straddled him and began massaging his chest. Her hands felt so good that he didn't resist. "Brianne Davenport collects sports cars."

"Where did you hear that?" Joshua asked.

"She told Donny when she was hitting on him. She invited him to take one for a spin."

Clasping her hands, Joshua gazed into her eyes. "She invited my sixteen-year-old son to take one of her sports cars for spin?"

"I think between the lines she was asking him to take her for a spin."

"I wonder if she has a Ferrari," he said.

With a gasp, Cameron recalled Brianne telling Donny that she owned a Ferrari. "Cheryl had Brianne's direct line number in her pocket. The two of them used to be friends. She had to know that Brianne collected sports cars." With each point she made, she stabbed him in the chest with her fingernail.

He grasped her finger and kissed it. "Cheryl was desperate to get out of the country, and probably for a fix. She had a hundred-thousand dollar sports car."

She moved in closer. "Cheryl had that phone number for Brianne Davenport because she was trying to unload the Ferrari to make her getaway." She scratched her head. "Why come all the way back here to Chester and Hookstown from Vegas? She could have unloaded that car a thousand places between Vegas and here. She had no family here. What drew her here?"

Deep in thought, Joshua said more to himself, "Maybe after all those years in Hollywood making movies, with the likes of people like Humphrey Phoenix, she thought the only people she could count on and trust to help her were those friends she had back home."

"Only she ended up being wrong."

"Which friend killed her?" he asked humorlessly. "The manipulative cougar, the cheating husband, or the bitter computer geek?"

"We need to get someone to talk to us." Cameron pressed her forehead against his.

"Which one?"

"How about Donny's girlfriend?"

"Kaden?" Joshua asked.

"Brianne Davenport."

"She's not his girlfriend." Joshua whispered into her ear.

"You tell her that," she whispered into his. "I want to set a trap."

Her hot breath on his neck sent a shiver all the way down his spine. "What kind of trap are you talking about?" He kissed her.

"A good one." She brushed her fingers across his cheek. "I want to use your son for bait."

They were startled by the clearing of a throat. Joshua almost knocked her out of his lap when he rolled over to see Donny smirking at them in the doorway with his arms folded across his chest. "So this is what you do when you're home alone while I'm at school."

# Chapter Thirteen

"Dad, I know where to find the VIN number." Donny did the teenaged eye-roll when Joshua asked him for the fifth time about locating the vehicle identification number on Brianne's Ferrari.

In spite of Cameron's assurances of protection, including an ear mike, Joshua didn't like the idea of using Donny to find and determine if Brianne Davenport had Cheryl Smith's Ferrari.

A search of DMV records showed that the VIN number for Brianne's Ferrari wasn't a match for Cheryl Smith's car. However, for the right amount of money, and with the right connections, a VIN number can be swapped for a similar car.

Without any proof that Brianne had possession of the Ferrari belonging to the murder victim, Cameron couldn't get a court order to examine her car.

So Donny was going in.

Joshua didn't like it one bit.

Cameron and Joshua had listened in on the phone when Donny called the winery owner under the pretense of asking her for a part-time job after school and on weekends.

While Joshua was surprised, Cameron wasn't when she offered the teenager a job without asking about his skills, experience, or references. "When can you start?" Brianne asked.

Donny came back with the question, "What kind of work do you want me to do?"

Her laugh was husky. "I need a new gopher."

"Gopher?" he replied. "What's a gopher?"

"You go-for this and go-for that." She elaborated, "You'll be my personal assistant."

Cameron wrote a note for Joshua to read. "Freddie? What happened?"

After setting up an appointment for Donny to meet her at the winery for an interview the next day after school, they hung up. With a wide grin, he turned around to ask them how he had done in setting up "the sting."

While Cameron suppressed her laughter, Joshua explained, "This is not a sting. A sting is what con artists do to marks. We're not con artists, and Brianne Davenport is not a mark."

"Then what is this?" Donny asked.

"This is an investigation, and you're going in undercover to collect evidence so that I can get a search warrant," said Cameron.

Donny's eyes brightened. "Undercover. I like that. That's better than working a sting." With a bounce in his step, he left the study and jogged up the stairs to his room.

Joshua dropped into the chair behind his desk. "I'm glad he likes it because I don't. I have a bad feeling about this whole thing."

"He's got you and me and two state troopers watching his back," she said. "What could go wrong?"

They met Cameron at her office at the state police barracks located in Raccoon Township in Pennsylvania. While Irving snoozed in her chair behind her desk, Cameron inserted the ear bud into Donny's ear and gave him last minute instructions.

"We can hear everything you and Mrs. Davenport say," she warned him.

"And do," Joshua added from where he sat on the corner of Cameron's desk.

"Don't worry, Dad," Donny said, "I have a girlfriend. Mrs. Davenport is really sexy, but she's old, too."

"So was Mrs. Robinson." Cameron referred to the older woman in *The Graduate*, a late 1960's movie starring Anne Bancroft as an older married woman who seduces a young Dustin Hoffman into an affair.

"Who's Mrs. Robinson?" Donny asked. "Is she another suspect? Will I get to go undercover again after this?"

"You explain it to him," she directed Joshua before turning to the two troopers waiting for her direction. "We need to stay close with this one."

❧ ❧ ❧ ❧

One advantage of a stakeout in a rural area is that there are innumerable places to hide. While Donny was driving his father's SUV up the winding drive to the estate home on the top of the hill of Davenport Wineries, Cameron was maneuvering her cruiser along a dirt road that led to an old spring house behind the estate. If there was any trouble, it was a hop over a fence and a jog through a vineyard behind the main house to the garage.

The cruiser was a loaner from the motor pool until they fumigated hers. It had been two days since the skunk attack and all she had received from the motor pool was a stuffed toy skunk left on her desk.

"Not that I expect there to be any trouble," Cameron assured Joshua to ease his nerves. "All he has to do is ask if he can take her Ferrari for a spin. He looks under the hood when she shows it to him, which all young men like to do; and then snap a picture of the VIN number with his cell phone, and send it to me to compare with the VIN to Cheryl's car." She smiled. "How easy is that?"

"Can you stop talking?" Joshua was staring straight ahead to the back of the Davenport house. "The more you tell me how easy it is, the more nervous I get." He shook his head. "I have a really bad feeling about this. What happened to Freddie?"

"He probably quit because he got tired of sleeping with an older woman ... even if she is hot." Cameron reached across the front of the cruiser to pat his leg. "Donny is going to be fine."

He turned to her. His eyes narrowed to blue slits.

She pulled back her hand. "I'll stop talking."

"Thank you."

Brianne's voice through the speaker sounded as breathlessly excited as a child seeing a long awaited birthday present come through the door when she greeted Donny. After some small talk while she showed him around the mansion, she confessed, "I was surprised when you called me. I had heard you had a girlfriend."

"I do," Donny replied.

During the moment of silence, Cameron cursed into her mike. "Wrong answer, Donny. Now she thinks you really are looking for a job. Let her know that you're willing to play the field. She has to think you're interested in her."

"She's not really my girlfriend," he backtracked. "We go out and kiss and stuff, but we still see other people."

"What kind of stuff?" Joshua asked.

Brianne's voice moved in closer and grew deeper. "I'm glad to hear that. You had me worried there for a minute."

There was a long moment of silence and the sound of movement, followed by a kiss.

Cameron saw Joshua shift uncomfortably in his seat. She jerked around when she saw him pull his gun out from where he had it concealed under his jacket.

Over the years of encountering one deadly case after another, Joshua learned to never be without his semi-automatic Berretta handgun within easy reach. He checked the chamber.

"What are you going to do?" she asked. "Shoot Brianne? All she's doing is kissing him."

"I've got a very bad feeling," he said. "It keeps getting worse."

"Do I have the job?" Donny asked.

She laughed. "Don't you even want to know what I'm paying you?"

"Sure. How much?"

"Five thousand dollars a month."

"What?" Donny and Cameron gasped in unison.

Brianne continued laughing. "Let's get started. We'll start in the bedroom."

When Joshua grabbed the door handle, she grabbed his wrist. "Wait!"

"Can I see your cars first?" Donny asked with the eagerness of boyish youth. "You promised that I could drive one."

"Yes, I did." Brianne sounded disappointed. "Okay. They're out in the garage. I have more than a half-dozen beauties, and there are plenty of roads that we can turn them out on at high speed. I'll let you take your pick. Would you like a Corvette, Porsche, Jaguar—"

"Didn't you tell me that you had a Ferrari?"

Cameron and Joshua held their breath while waiting for her answer.

There was a silence while Brianne seemed to gauge her response. "Yes, as a matter of fact, I do have one."

"I've always wanted to drive a Ferrari," Donny said. "I've only seen pictures of them, but never have seen one up close and live."

His excitement seemed to calm her nerves. "I guess there's no time like the present."

Cameron set her phone on the top of her laptop along with the VIN number they were looking for.

"All he has to do is take the picture of the VIN," Joshua muttered. "Then he gets out of there."

"What if she locks the garage and won't let him out until he gives her a sample of his work?" When she saw his dead-panned expression she said, "It's a joke, Josh. She isn't really going to lock him in there."

"Are you sure about that?"

An echo in their voices indicated that they were now in the garage.

"Wow!" Donny shouted. "I've never seen so many fancy rides in one place, except on television. And they're all red."

"What can I say?" Brianne replied. "I look good in red. You should see me in my red lingerie."

"Will you look under the hood already, Donny?" Joshua pleaded.

"Can I check it out under the hood?" Donny asked.

"Be my guess," Brianne replied.

They heard a pop like a hood being raised on a car. Brianne rattled off the size of the engine and other specs that would impress any car buff.

"Do you mind if I take a picture of it to show my friends?" Donny told her that his friends would never believe him otherwise.

After she had granted him permission, Cameron snatched up her phone to watch for the close-up image of the vehicle identification number on the engine of the Ferrari. "Got it." She held up the picture to the long number she had.

"Ready to take it for—" Brianne's invitation was cut off by a scream, followed by a shriek and grunt from Donny.

"Move in!" Cameron called out across the mike to the troopers. "It's gone bad. Move in!"

Joshua didn't hear her order. He was already out of the cruiser and over the fence.

By the time Cameron had cleared the fence, Joshua had turned the corner of the garage with his gun drawn. The siren from the troopers screamed while they made their way up the twisted driveway.

Joshua estimated them to be one minute out. That was one minute too long. Inside the garage, he could hear Brianne screaming and begging hysterically. He found out why when he went in through the garage door to find that Freddie had taken Donny hostage, and was holding a box cutter to his throat.

Freddie's complexion was deathly white with dark circles around his red rimmed eyes that were wide with crazed anger.

Joshua barged in with his gun drawn and his finger on the trigger. "Drop the razor, Freddie!"

"Don't!" Brianne screamed when he moved in on his target. "He's going to kill him! He means it!"

"Drop it, Freddie!" Cameron yelled from behind Joshua.

"You mean like she dropped me?" Freddie hissed into Donny's ear. "Like she'll dump you as soon as another young beefcake looking for an older woman to show him the way crosses her path." He cried out, "I loved you!"

Brianne shrieked.

He muttered into Donny's ear, "Then she tossed me out like I was yesterday's garbage. Do you have any idea how that feels?"

"Hey, all I wanted was a ride in her car, man! I wasn't look for—"

"It feels like agony!"

"So get yourself a new girl," Donny suggested.

"I loved her!" Freddie gritted his teeth. "I'm going to save you the agony … and let her watch me do it."

"No!" Brianne screamed through her tears.

"Dad!"

"I'm here, son. He's not going to do it." Joshua could see Donny fighting to keep the tears from his eyes. There was no way his son was going to let any of them see him cry.

"Who's going to stop me, Daddy?" Freddie asked with a wild laugh.

"Me."

Freddie pulled Donny in closer and pressed the blade tighter against his throat. "Do you really have the balls to take the chance of shooting your own son?"

"Somebody do something!" Brianne screamed. "He's going to kill him."

"Josh …" Cameron whispered behind him. "I'll let you make the call."

Joshua's eyes met his son's.

Donny took a deep breath.

Joshua could see Donny's lips move. He pressed his finger against the trigger.

*One.*

*Two.*

*Three.*

Donny jerked to the left, away from the razor.

Joshua pulled the trigger. Advancing, he pulled it again, and again, and again.

The first bullet tore through the forearm of the arm holding the blade before hitting Freddie in the shoulder. The shot was enough to free Donny for him to plunge to the floor. The second and third bullets hit Freddie in the chest. As he fell, the fourth bullet hit him between the eyes and came out the back of his head to splatter his brains across the front of a freezer behind him.

"Are you okay?" Joshua checked Donny's neck. There was a small cut where Freddie had the blade pressed against it.

"Someone just tried to kill me. How do you think I am?" Donny was breathing heavily, a technique he used when playing football to keep his nerves under control.

Joshua wrapped his arm around his shoulders. Warning him not to hug him there, in front of everyone, Donny shot him a look.

When he felt his son tremble, Joshua said, "Let's go home, son."

"Four shots fired, and four hit their targets," Cameron reported to them. "I'm impressed with how you pulled that off."

She saw that Brianne was already holding onto the younger of the two troopers, the more attractive of the two, for all it was worth. She was dressed in a slinky, ultra-short black dress with red high heels for Donny's job interview.

*I guess if you have it, flaunt it.*

"I'm taking Donny home," Joshua told Cameron.

"Josh—"

"Not now," he interrupted her with a sharp tone that startled her.

One of the troopers said, "We need to get their statements."

Cameron said, "I'm the lead in this case. They'll give their statements later."

"But—"

"Later!" As Joshua and Donny passed her, she called out, "You did good, Donny. You're a chip off the old block."

Donny slipped his arm around his father's back. "Thanks, Cam. That means a lot. He taught me everything I know."

Searching for a sign from Joshua that he didn't blame her for what had almost happened, Cameron watched them turn the corner of the garage. He gave her nothing. Not even so much as a glance over his shoulder in her direction.

*You really blew it this time, babe. Best thing to ever come your way, and you blew it by putting his son in the direct path of a murder investigation. What were you thinking? Josh tried to tell you. He kept saying it was too easy. When it seems too easy, that's when you need to really be on your toes—like pulling over a car for a broken turn signal. You think you're just giving someone a warning about getting his car fixed, and the next thing you know your new bride is a widow. You let your guard down, Cam, and almost got your silver fox's son killed.*

Squinting to fight the tears coming to her eyes, Cameron sighed deeply and turned around to look over at Freddie's body. He had bled out all over the floor. His hair, brains, and blood were splattered across the front of a freezer to resemble a psychiatrist's inkblot test.

*Freezer? In the garage?*

Cameron whirled around to Brianne. "What's that freezer doing here?"

"What? Is there a law against having a freezer in your garage now?"

"Answer the question." She rushed over at Brianne. When she realized how close she was to taking out her anger on her, the detective stopped short.

Her charge was enough to scare the attitude out of Brianne. "It's broken. The landscaper keeps some of the gardening supplies that are particularly attractive to rodents and raccoons in here. Since it's airtight, everything stays fresh longer." Her attitude returning, she put her hands on her slender hips. "Any other questions?"

"You'll get the rest of my questions down at the station."

# Chapter Fourteen

At the state police barracks, Lieutenant Miles Dugan was waiting for Cameron in her office after she had Brianne escorted to the interrogation room. With her chief leaning against the corner of her desk with his arms folded across his chest, and Irving sitting up straight with his emerald eyes squinting at her; Cameron had no doubt but that she was going to get it with both barrels.

Irving was in a snit because she had left him behind to go off with Joshua.

Lieutenant Dugan was furious about her simple uncover assignment ending with a dead body. "What happened out there, Gates?"

"You wouldn't be asking me that if you didn't hear already." Cameron stepped around him to offer Irving a pet, which the cat rejected with a jerk of his head before jumping back into her chair to leave her no place to sit.

Dugan unfolded his arms and placed his hands on his hips. In doing so, he pulled back his suit jacket to reveal his lieutenant's shield and gun. "*You* were supposed to be in charge."

"I was in charge."

"Not according to the officers," her chief said. "When it turned bad, you were heard to say to the civilian you brought along for a ride that it was his call. He put four bullets into the suspect—"

"Who was holding a razor to his son's throat."

"Exactly," Dugan said. "You let a victim's family member take over. Thornton was the last person to hand off the lead to. Hell! He shouldn't have even been there."

"Joshua Thornton isn't exactly a civilian," Cameron said. "He's the prosecuting attorney—"

"A legal weenie."

"No, he's not," Cameron said. "Thornton has a long history of criminal investigation with the military and federal government. He's fully trained in law enforcement. He's got more experience than half of the troopers we have out in the field."

His glare cut her off. "Joshua Thornton may be a big shot over in West Virginia, but not here in my jurisdiction." He pointed to the floor. "Here, my detectives are in charge—always. They don't hand over the lead to civilians, no matter who they are. When Joshua Thornton crosses that state line, he's just like everybody else. He shoots someone, you bring him in. You don't send him home with a 'see you later, honey.'"

"I don't call him 'honey.'" Cameron hung her head. "I take full responsibility for what happened. I never should have brought Joshua's son into this investigation in the first place."

"If you're looking for an argument, you won't get it from me." His hard face softened. "How's the boy?"

Not knowing the answer to his question, she held her breath before shaking her head and shrugging her shoulders. "I don't know. Physically, he's fine." She added more to assure herself, "Donny's tough like his dad."

"And you and his dad? How are you two?"

"I have no idea."

Lieutenant Dugan patted her on the shoulder. "Make sure Thornton, both of them, get in here first thing in the morning to give their statements. Meanwhile, I have to go put a call into *our* prosecutor's office to give him the lowdown."

The smile he shot her before going to his office did little to assure her that things were going to be fine on all fronts. She had not only lost control, but had handed it off to someone else in front of the uniformed officers.

*How stupid can you be, Gates?*

If it had been anyone but Donny whose life was on the line, she would have held onto the lead with a vice-like grip. She couldn't hold onto it with it being Donny. If she had made the call and it ended badly, then Joshua would never have been able to forgive her. It was a risk she couldn't take—didn't want to take.

Even if Lieutenant Dugan and her colleagues understood her reasoning, it was a bad call. *Now they think I'm a weak, indecisive woman who needs to let her man run the show. It's going to take forever to win back their respect. They may never fumigate my cruiser after this.*

She still saw Joshua's back turned to her when he led Donny home. *What Joshua must be thinking about me now.*

Cringing at what she imagined was going through Joshua's mind, Cameron turned to Irving. Their eyes met. "Go ahead, Irving," she said. "Let me have it."

With a jerk of his head, Irving turned his back to her and curled up on her chair.

*Even my cat's mad at me.*

Brianne slammed her hand down flat on the table top in the interview room when Cameron came in with a case file tucked under her arm. "What the hell is going on? I'm the victim, and I'm being treated like I'd killed someone."

"Maybe you did." Cameron slipped into the chair across from her. The table was so small that her knees touched Brianne's on the other side.

The detective's intrusion into her space made Brianne back away from the table. "What are you talking about? You were there. Freddie flipped out because I fired him."

"To replace him as your boy toy with a sixteen-year-old boy." She leaned in. "Freddie was only twenty years old, and you chewed him up and spit him out like used up chewing gum."

"You make Freddie sound like a kid," Brianne said. "There are men two years younger than him overseas killing people. Freddie knew exactly what he was doing."

"You toyed with his emotions before he was old enough to know how to handle it," the detective said. "When you play with the emotions of someone who is too immature or stable to handle it, then people get hurt. You might as well have shot him yourself."

The corners of Brianne's lips curled. "Judge me all you want, but Freddie was of legal age." She stood up.

"Sit down!"

The command in Cameron's voice made Brianne drop back down into the chair. With a steely look in her light brown eyes, the detective opened the folder and took out a picture of the Ferrari's VIN number. She slid it across the table to her. "Recognize this?"

"It's a VIN number on a car engine." With a shrug of her shoulders, she slid the picture back across the table.

"That's the photograph Donny took of the VIN number from the Ferrari that is right now in *your* garage—the Ferrari *you* claim to be yours." Cameron slipped a police report from the folder and slid it, along with the picture, over to land in front of Brianne. "This is the VIN number belonging to the Ferrari that Humphrey Phoenix had given Cherry Pickens, also known as Cheryl Smith, as a gift. It is the Ferrari that she drove out of Vegas back in May 1985. That Ferrari disappeared the same time she did." She tapped both numbers with her index fingers. "They're a match. The Ferrari that is in your garage was Cheryl Smith's car. She was murdered, and you now have her car." Leaving the facts in front of her, Cameron sat back in her seat. "You told me that you hadn't seen Cheryl since before she took off in 1978. If that's true, how is it that you have her car? Explain that to me."

The two women sat in silence.

Brianne stared at the picture and the VIN number in front of her.

Cameron engaged in silence contests the way other people engaged in staring contests. Whoever broke the silence lost the game. The amoral type of suspects could play the game almost as good as she could.

Almost.

"I guess Donny didn't really want to come work for me."

"Seriously?" Cameron smiled. "He's sixteen years old. He's got a girlfriend, and she's got an eleven-thirty curfew."

"I can stay out all night, and I could have taught him so much—"

"Get your mind out of the gutter." Cameron slammed her hand on top of the pictures. "Cheryl Smith came to see you. She had your phone number in her pocket. That Ferrari is proof that you saw her. She was a key suspect in killing your best friend. That gave you motive for killing her. Now, unless you can give me something to prove you didn't kill her, I believe I have enough to take this to the prosecutor, to take to the grand jury, and bring you up on charges of murder."

"Murder?" Brianne now appeared insulted.

"Murder."

"Now wait a minute, I didn't kill Cheryl. She did come to the winery to see me, but I never saw her. I wasn't there."

"Then how did you get her car? How did she get your business card?"

"Kyle gave the card to her."

"Kyle? Angie's fiancé?" Cameron was doubtful.

Brianne nodded her head. "He told me that she had stopped by and wanted to know if I would be interested in buying her Ferrari, cheap—something like fifty-thousand dollars. Wow! A Ferrari that was fully loaded for only fifty-thousand dollars? Kyle knew me well enough to know I'd snap that up, so he told her he would pass on the information, which he did. He said he asked her for her phone number, but she wouldn't give him one. This was before cell phones. So he gave her my business card and told her to call me the next morning."

"And so she called you …"

"No, she didn't." Brianne sat up in her seat and tapped the table top with her finger. "I never even spoke to Cheryl. I'm telling the truth. I never saw her, and I never spoke to her."

"How did you end up with the car?" Cameron asked.

Making her point, Brianne gestured wildly with both of her hands. "It was there in the driveway when I got to the office the next morning. The keys were even in the ignition. I looked it over. Took it for a spin. It was in pristine condition. Clean as a whistle. I waited for her to call." She nodded her head quickly. "Yeah, I wanted the car. I would have paid the fifty thousand—cash—but she never did call. After a few days, I put the car in the garage. Ned used some of his contacts at the track to get me a VIN number and a title so that I could register it with the DMV."

She leaned across the table at Cameron. "I swear! I never did see Cheryl when she was here. You have to believe me."

Cameron gazed at Brianne, who gazed back at her. The arrogant attitude that had been there when they started the interrogation was now gone. The detective had scared it out of her. "What about Ned?"

"Huh?" Brianne blinked her eyes.

"Ned? Cheryl had his phone number on the back of your business card. Did he see her?"

"He said he didn't. I remember asking him at the time. Of course, he could have been lying. I wouldn't put it past him hooking up with her for old-time's sake." She shrugged. "You need to ask him about that."

"Cheryl did hook up with someone shortly before she died," Cameron said.

"Could have been Ned."

"That's what I thought. But we got a court order for his DNA and it turned out not to be a match." The detective cocked her head at her. "Can you think of anyone else she could have hooked up with?"

"Nope."

The detective could feel Brianne's heavily made-up eyes begging for her to give some indication that she believed her.

Cameron replayed what she had gathered about Cheryl's return to town. So far, no one claimed to ever see her. It was as if she had blown in like the wind—only to have her presence felt—but not to be seen by anyone.

Now, Brianne was saying Kyle had given Cheryl the business card. Kyle claimed he hadn't seen her. Obviously, he was lying.

*I hate it when people lie to me.*

"Tell me about Kyle and Cheryl?" Cameron asked.

"Kyle and Cheryl?" Brianne laughed.

"Ned told me something about them having a roll in the hay, which caused Angie to break up with Kyle."

Brianne's cheeks turned pink. "Cheryl was wicked like that. She knew she had the power to manipulate men. She'd seduce someone she had no interest in just for the thrill of controlling them, and then she'd break their hearts the next day."

"Sounds horrible."

"She was awful."

Cameron squinted at her. "You'd never do anything like that." Her tone oozed with sarcasm. "Wound someone so badly that they'd lose their mind and end up dead?"

Brianne bit off each word. "Freddie's death is not my fault."

"If that's what you have to tell yourself to look in the mirror in the morning, so be it," Cameron said. "Tell me about Kyle. I thought he was head over heels in love with Angie. How is it that Cheryl was able to seduce him?"

"It was simple," Brianne said. "Angie refused to put out. Cheryl did. She needed a research paper to pass history, and she needed a really good grade. So, she seduced Kyle into writing it for her. For laughs, she tape recorded it. Then, after she got her grade, she gave the tape to Angie, who broke up with Kyle."

"Talk about a double whammy," Cameron said. "Not only did Cheryl use him to pass history, but she betrayed him and broke up his relationship with Angie."

Brianne laughed when she said, "Kyle *hated* Cheryl for that."

"But then Angie took him back," Cameron said.

Covering her mouth, Brianne giggled.

"Or didn't she?"

"What are you asking for? Kyle's fantasy or the reality?"

"Kyle claims they got engaged the same night she disappeared. Angie still had the engagement ring on her finger when her body was recovered."

"Oh, yeah, so I heard that," Brianne replied. "Kyle has been playing the King of Broken Hearts ever since that night. First, it started with they got engaged. Then, as time went on and he got a taste of pity, it was they got engaged and even set a date. After Angie's body was found, their last night together had turned into a full-blown declaration of love in which she gave him her virginity."

"So I heard." Cameron recalled Kyle's tearful story of that night he and Angie had gotten engaged. "Are you saying that isn't what you think happened?"

She laughed. "It's a bunch of bull. Angie was one of those old-fashioned girls. Plus, she was terrified of getting pregnant and ending up like her mother—hiding behind a lie. There was no way Angie was going to give it up before her wedding night. That whole story Kyle tells about them giving themselves to each other that night is nothing but a fantasy that he's made up in his mind." She shrugged. "What's really sad is, I think he actually believes it."

Cameron wished that there was some way the autopsy could reveal if Angie had sexual relations shortly before her death. Unfortunately, after years in the water, her body was too badly decomposed to tell. Her mind whirled with visions of Kyle killing the love of his life after being rejected. "Would Angie have accepted the ring from Kyle?"

"That part I think is true." Brianne nodded her head. "We knew Kyle was planning to pop the question that night. He had told someone, and word got around. Angie had no idea what she was going to say. She spent the good part of the evening avoiding him. But then, Cheryl and her friends started. Angie had about all that she could handle. After the rink closed, and we were out in the parking lot, I remember seeing Kyle coming out to join us, and I asked her what she was going to tell him. She was whipped. She did not feel like dealing with that at the moment. Ned and I tried to talk her into letting us go along with them so that they wouldn't' be alone for Kyle to pop the question, but he was so insistent." She concluded, "I think Angie took the ring for the time being until she could find a way to break it off."

"You think?"

Brianne shrugged her shoulders. "I always assumed that was how she ended up with it. I could see it happening that way."

"Or maybe Kyle put the ring on Angie's finger after killing her when she turned him down," Cameron said.

"I could see it happening that way, too," Brianne's tone was matter-of-fact.

# CHAPTER FIFTEEN

Cameron hated believing Brianne. As much as she hated it, her story was too unbelievable for her not to believe it. *How many people go to work and find a Ferrari, keys in the ignition, abandoned in their parking space?*

As anxious as she was to go to Joshua's house and check on Donny, she needed to make a stop at Doris Sullivan's farm first.

In the passenger seat of the cruiser, Irving was making it known that he was ready to go home for dinner or bed, or both, with his loud meows while peering out the window.

"This will only take a minute, Irving," she told him, "and then we'll be at Joshua's in twenty minutes, and you can start glaring at him."

Irving let go with a feline version of a howl, which reminded Cameron of an opera singer on steroids.

"You need to get over your jealousy of Joshua." She shook her finger at the cat.

Irving lifted his face to her. *Rawl!* She heard "no."

"Doesn't matter anyway." Her tone was filled with misery. "I wouldn't be surprised if Joshua doesn't shoot me when I come through his door—and I wouldn't blame him."

Doris Sullivan's long, gravel driveway was blocked by fire trucks and county police vehicles. The flames spilled out of the ground floor of the farmhouse and snaked up the walls to the roof. After bringing her SUV to a halt at the end of the line of emergency crews, Cameron ordered Irving to stay put and jumped out of the car. She jogged up the road to the police who were trying to hold back spectators. They parted to let her through after she flashed her police shield.

"What happened?" she called to a uniformed officer she recognized.

"Can't you smell the gasoline?" he replied. "Arson."

"Did you get Doris Sullivan out?"

He pointed to where the EMTs were loading her on a stretcher into the back of an ambulance. "Found her alive but unconscious where she had jumped out the second floor window."

A call came out among the fire fighters around the house. "You! Halt! Come back here!"

A naked man darted out from behind a lilac bush to sprint across the back yard to a pasture. He was running as fast as his legs could carry him. Caught in the beam of a police cruiser's spotlight, he continued to run in all his glory while several police officers and Cameron chased after him. She managed to close-in behind him. At the pasture fence, the escapee attempted to scale it when she tackled him down to the ground.

When she realized she was pinning a naked man to the ground, Cameron pulled up. When the flashlight beams illuminated his face, she recognized the runner as Ralph Hildebrand, who was not only naked, but completely aroused. Caught off guard by the pressure of Ralph's erect penis in her ribs, she not only pulled back, but jumped to her feet.

Freed, the elderly man tried to cover himself as best he could while the group, all men except for one, stared down at him. Those men who didn't turn away in embarrassment laughed.

"Ralph! What are you doing here?" Cameron asked while looking straight ahead at the fence from which she had pulled the escapee down. "Give him your coat," she ordered one of the officers.

Laughing, the officer shook his head. "You give him your coat, detective."

Looking straight down at him, she repeated her question. "Ralph, Mildred told us you were on a business trip."

The old man pleaded, "You're not going to tell her, are you? You don't know what that woman is capable of."

❧ ❧ ❧ ❧

Doris Sullivan didn't fare the jump from the second story as well as her house guest. Instead of her fall being cushioned by bushes, she suffered a concussion, broke her arm, and several ribs. She had to be carted away in the ambulance. Before going to the hospital to question her about the fire and the possibility of it being connected to Cheryl's and Angie's murders, Cameron tried to find out Ralph's side of the story.

In the back of an ambulance, Ralph, wrapped in a blanket, apologized to her for the aroused state that refused to diminish. "It will be at least another hour before the medication will wear off," he whispered.

She whispered back, "You take male enhancement drugs?"

A low chuckle escaped his lips. "It's to be expected that as a man gets older …" He caught her eye. "I call them my best friends."

"I'm sure you do." An edge of sarcasm crept into her voice. The fact that Ralph not only cheated on his wife, but used drugs to help, further disgusted her. "The fire chief is already calling this arson. Someone tried to kill Doris, and maybe you. Can you think of who would want to do that?"

"No one knows I'm in town."

"What about your friend?"

"Do you mean my pills?"

"Not your best friends," Cameron clarified. "Your female friend."

"Doris? Why would Doris set fire to her own house?"

"I mean your *other* female friend. What's her name?"

"Oh!" he shouted with a wave of the blanket that revealed his condition to her again. "You mean Peggy."

"What happened to Peggy?"

"She became a pain in the butt," Ralph said. "That's the problem with most women. After a while, they assume I'm going to divorce Mildred and marry them. Why would they think such a thing?"

"Did it ever occur to you that after an extended period of drinking the milk for free that the farmer would assume the customer would like to buy the cow?" she asked.

"Why should I buy the cow when I can get the milk for free?" he challenged her.

Around the corner of the ambulance, Cameron could see Irving glaring at her from the rear window of her cruiser. As amusing as the debate with Ralph was, she had to get moving.

*Ralph thinks Mildred is dangerous to tick off. No one is as ruthless as a cat when it comes to missing dinner.*

She sighed and turned away from Irving's glare to keep focused on the case. "Tell me about what happened tonight."

"You tell me," he said. "Doris and I were enjoying each other's company upstairs, and suddenly, she started yelling about how things were on fire. I thought she was talking about my performance. Next thing I know, she's pushing me off her and throwing open the window and jumping out."

"Do you think Mildred did this?" Cameron asked.

He scratched his head. "Mildred did tell me that if I didn't cut it out that I was going to burn in hell. But I told her

I was still out of town." He snapped his fingers. "Peggy! She's crazy! I wouldn't be surprised if she wasn't one of those stalker-types." He looked both ways as if searching for his ex-mistress. "I did have a feeling that I was being followed when I drove out here this afternoon."

"What was Peggy's reaction when you told her that you weren't going to leave Mildred?" Cameron asked. "Was she upset?"

Ralph gestured at the burning house. "Take a look. What do you think?"

"Then, I'll have a talk with Peggy." She bent over him. Amusement crept into her voice when she asked, "How long has this been going on between you and Doris Sullivan?"

Ralph looked around before a cocky grin crossed his face. "Do you want to know the truth?"

"If you can manage that."

Missing her sarcastic tone, he answered, "It never ended."

"Do you mean …"

"Can you believe one man can get so lucky?" He chuckled. "I have the best of all worlds. Two women. Both in love with me. The one has a daddy who is just itching to marry off his daughter and set his son-in-law up in business. She really doesn't care what I do as long as I bring home the bacon and keep up appearances. The other woman is a spit-fire between the sheets, and the last thing she wants is any man telling her what to do." He giggled so hard he had to stop to catch his breath.

"So you never did have to choose between the two of them," she said.

"Mildred likes to think I chose her." Ralph leaned toward her.

Aware of his still aroused condition staring up at her from under the blanket, she backed up a step.

"Truth is," he said, "I chose Doris, but she turned me down. Next thing I know, her folks sent her off to some boarding school someplace. Mildred was on my case. She was fast approaching eighteen, at which point she'd turn into an old maid, and her father was welcoming me into the family business—so I married her. A year later, Doris is back and hell—I won the lottery!"

Cameron cocked her head at him. "And what about Angie?"

"What about Angie?"

"Did you buy the story that Angie was Doris' sister?"

The wicked grin fell from Ralph's face. "I may be a bastard, but I'm not a stupid bastard. I knew. But Doris said I didn't have to take any responsibility for her. She would raise her as her sister. But then her parents got killed in that car accident, and Doris really did have to be her mother. Still, she said she needed and wanted nothing from me. Then, Angie wanted to know who her father was."

"Did Doris tell her about you?"

"She asked me about it." Ralph wiped his nose with the blanket. "Yeah, I'm a real piece of work. I admit it. I begged her not to tell Angie about me. I wasn't thinking about her. All I could think about was what Mildred would do if it got out that her husband had fathered another woman's child. She's always so worried about what her friends will think." He sighed. "I told Doris to tell Angie that her father was dead. So she did."

The lights inside the back of the ambulance lit up the tears that seeped into his eyes. "Never occurred to me that poor girl, my baby girl, would die thinking that her daddy was dead." He sniffed. "Guess it's better than knowing that he was a real-life bastard."

# Chapter Sixteen

Through the sun porch door, Cameron watched Joshua spooning vanilla ice cream into a bowl. She could see that his skin was still moist from a shower. Wet, his silver hair fell in loose, wavy locks down the back of his neck. In his bathrobe and lounging pants, he was ready for bed.

*Rowlf!* Smelling the sweet, frozen, creamy dessert, Irving struggled out of her arms and darted through the dog door to trot over to the kitchen counter and rub against Joshua's leg.

"Oh, now we're friends." He gazed at her waiting on the other side of the kitchen door. "What are you waiting for? Suddenly, you're going to start knocking and waiting for me to come open the door for you?"

Still tentative, she opened the door. "Am I allowed to come in?"

Joshua's silver eyebrows met in the middle of his forehead. "Why wouldn't you be?"

She crossed the kitchen to wrap her arms around his waist. "You had me so scared." She rested her head against his warm bare chest. His clean musky scent excited her senses. She could feel his heart beat against her ear. "When you didn't say anything to me—"

Hugging her, he rocked her in his arms. "I had to get Donny home. He was really upset, and he didn't want to start bawling there in front of those troopers and Brianne. I had to get him out of there."

She uttered a heavy sigh. "So it's not over."

His chuckle seemed to echo in her ear where it was pressed against his chest. "Of course not." He pushed her away from him. Holding onto her shoulders, he peered into her eyes. "Do you have any idea how important you are to me?"

Her lips curled. "No. Tell me."

"I love you … more than you will ever know."

She cocked her head at him while he waited for her response. "You're not so bad yourself."

He grabbed her and kissed her so hard on the lips that their teeth crashed against each other. She could feel his passion for her flow through her body like a wave of emotion. When he let her up for air, she gasped out, "I love you, too, Joshua Thornton." She threw her arms around him, and held onto him as tight as she could. "Come here."

Joshua didn't realize that he had fallen asleep until Irving began licking his cheek where a miniscule drop of ice cream had dried. Half-conscious, he swatted at what he thought was a fly before realizing that it was the skunk cat. "Get away from me."

"Who are you talking to?" Cameron asked from where she was wrapped around his naked body.

They were wrapped around each other under a comforter taken from a linen closet in the downstairs family room.

Now awake, Joshua remembered the night before. After they were certain Donny had gone to bed, they had sneaked down to the family room. Giggling like a couple of guilty teenagers, they had built a fire in the fireplace and made love on the floor under an old comforter.

"Irving's bothering me," he told her while coming to his senses.

"Irving," Cameron said, "leave him alone."

Chastised, Irving went over to jump up onto the sofa and curl up on top of Admiral, who had spent the night stretched out on something more comfortable.

"What were you telling me last night?" Joshua struggled to recall what little actual conversation they had the night before. He was too focused on staring into the depths of her eyes and kissing her lips to pay attention. "Doris has another freezer?"

"Now you want to talk about it." Hugging him tighter, she nuzzled his neck. "She has a freezer in her barn."

"Did you have a search warrant?"

"Someone tried to burn down her house with her and Ralph in it. I was looking for an arsonist."

"Sure you were," he laughed while hugging her.

"I found it right there in the feed room. It wasn't plugged in, just like the freezer that was in Brianne Davenport's garage. She uses it to store the horse feed in. That was where the freezer Cheryl Smith's body was stashed in came from. Forensics had found traces of molasses and oats in it. This freezer had a container of molasses and bags of oats."

Joshua said, "When I asked her about it, she pointed us in the direction of Mildred. She didn't think we'd find out about her having a second freezer."

Cameron put the scene together. "She killed Cheryl for revenge because she thought she had killed Angie, stuffed her in the old freezer, and hid it in Albert's basement. Then she had to get rid of the Ferrari. So she left it on Brianne's doorstep like an abandoned baby."

"How did she know Cheryl was in town?" Joshua asked.

"Kyle told her," she answered.

"I thought Kyle said he never saw Cheryl when she came back to town."

"Brianne told me that he did," she said. "She claims she never saw Cheryl either. But Kyle, who set up the computer system at the winery, was on the Davenport payroll in 1985. Brianne says he was the one who told her about Cheryl being in town and stopping by the winery to sell her the Ferrari."

"He must have been the one who gave her Brianne's business card with Ned's phone number on the back," he said. "Why would he lie?"

"Because he didn't want to be a suspect," she answered. "He knew she had been murdered. He also knew he had a strong motive. Not only did Cheryl destroy his relationship with Angie, but she was also the prime suspect in her murder. To admit that he saw her would be putting himself under the spotlight."

"Lying also puts him under the spotlight."

"I need to go question Ned Carter again," she said. "Now we know who gave Cheryl his phone number. Brianne says Cheryl never showed up, but her car did. I wonder if something odd like that happened to Ned. If I can recreate the chain of events leading up to and after Cheryl's murder, I might have luck in finding real evidence against Doris."

He rolled over onto his side and smiled at her. "So you think it's Doris?"

"Of course, I do. It was her freezer. I'll go to the hospital and question her today." Conscious of covering herself, she sat up. "What time is it?" She looked up at the anniversary clock on the mantle. It was six o'clock in the morning.

Remembering Joshua's son, who was only two floors above them in the house, she sprang for her clothes while clutching the comforter around her. "I have to go before Donny gets up and comes down here and finds us."

Her reminder woke Joshua up all the way. He dove for his clothes. "He's going to be up early. He and his friends are going to Pittsburgh for a concert. They're going out for brunch—"

"Dugan says you and Donny need to go into the police barracks to give them your—"

"Admiral!" Donny's voice called from upstairs. "Come on, boy! Do you want to go out?"

Clutching their clothes against their naked bodies, Joshua and Cameron froze. They held their breath. They could sense, rather than see, Donny at the top of the steps waiting for Admiral.

The huge dog took his time climbing down off the sofa to the floor and making his way up the stairs.

"There you are," Donny greeted him.

They watched the ceiling while listening to Donny's footsteps cross the floor to the back door to let the dog out. Then they followed the sound of his footsteps to the kitchen cupboard where he took out Admiral's dog food. The whirl of the can opener signaled the opening of the can.

With a loud meow, Irving flew off the top of the back of the sofa and up the steps.

"No!" Cameron gasped.

Joshua covered her mouth with his hand. "Shhh!"

"Irving, what are you doing here?" Donny asked.

A moment later, Irving trotted down the stairs with Donny behind him.

"Traitor," Joshua hissed at the cat.

A wide smile crossed Donny's face at the sight of his father and Cameron wrapped in a comforter after having spent the night together. "Well, well, well." Chuckling, he folded his arms across his chest. "Dad, I guess now would be a good time to talk to you about my curfew."

❧ ❧ ❧ ❧

"I don't understand the purposes of curfews anyway," Cameron argued with Joshua while he maneuvered the country roads in his SUV. "Like, what can Donny do after midnight that he can't do before?"

"It's called boundaries," Joshua grumbled. "Children need boundaries. I don't want my kids running around at all hours of the night getting into trouble."

"Oh, I can see Donny running around at all hours of the night getting into trouble," she said with sarcasm. "He's a good kid, Josh."

"And I want him to stay that way."

"Don't you think it's silly us hiding that we're intimate with each other from him?" she asked.

"It is now."

"I've spent the night before," she said.

"In the guest room."

She laughed. "That's the lie you tell Donny and he *knows* you're lying."

"Of course he does. We both just got caught with our pants down." He pointed a finger at her. "Your skunk cat is a snitch."

"You're only put out because he won't let you call him Irv." She wanted to further argue for Irving's innocence, but got distracted by a sharp turn that Joshua made to take his SUV down a worn country road leading back along a steep ridge in Johnsonville, a community on the outskirts of Chester. The back road was home to a row of mobile homes lots, one set up next to another. In an effort to make their trailers homier, their owners had erected wooden porches and decks with various degrees of success. Others had cheaply made additions that didn't match the original structure.

"Ralph's ex-mistress. Name, Peggy Lawson," she read the name in her report. "Lives at 15 Hickory Lane, located off Johnsonville Road."

Joshua pulled the SUV off the road. "There it is." He pointed to a yellow trailer with black shutters. A muddy, red sedan was parked in the gravel driveway next to a gardening shed. "Do you want me to come in with you?"

"Why do you think I brought you?" she asked.

"I came voluntarily because I need the mental exercise from arguing with you."

She smiled. "I'll do the questioning, and you'll be my back up."

Groaning, he shifted his car into drive. "Oh, I hope I don't have to shoot another suspect." He parked next to the sedan.

Cameron unclipped her police shield to show Ralph's ex-mistress when she answered the door. When she opened the passenger side door to climb out of the car, she saw two large gasoline cans filling the back seat of the sedan. The car reeked of the smell from the gasoline. "Josh?"

When she saw she had his attention, she pointed to the back seat of the car. He nodded his head. Together, they made their way up the steps to the front door. Standing aside from the doorway, Cameron knocked loudly on the door. "Peggy! It's the police. Will you please open the door?"

The response was silence.

Cameron knocked on the door again. "Peggy Lawson, open the door. We need to speak to you."

Joshua had his ear pressed to the side of the trailer. "I don't hear any movement." He turned the door knob, and it swung open.

Their guns drawn, Cameron entered first with Joshua directly behind her. With each turn they made, they aimed and searched the cluttered living room and kitchen area.

"I think someone was on a binge." With the muzzle of his gun, Joshua indicated a row of empty vodka bottles along the kitchen counter. There was only one glass next to the bottles. Spotting an empty cat food and water dish, he said, "She has a cat."

"She's not all bad."

"I wonder if her cat's a snitch."

"Peggy, it's the police," she announced again while peering down the hallway in case Peggy was asleep and didn't hear them entering. "We have some questions for you about Ralph Hildebrand and Doris Sullivan."

The hallway was too narrow to allow any place for her to hide. Cameron rushed down and threw open the door at the end of it.

The bedroom occupied the back portion of the home. The unmade king-sized bed filled the room, leaving barely enough space to navigate to the closet on the other side. Peggy Lawson was sprawled out on the bed with the sheets twisted around her naked body. An empty vodka bottle rested next to her body like a lover. Her hand still clutched the glass from which she had sipped.

Cameron holstered her gun.

"Is she alive?" Joshua asked in a low voice as if he feared waking her up. He was forced to wait in the hallway because there wasn't enough space for him to enter the room.

Cameron reached across the bed to feel Peggy's neck for a pulse. While searching, she watched her chest for any sign of breathing. She noticed her chest rise slightly. The pulse was very faint. "She's alive—barely!"

Joshua unclipped his phone from his belt and pressed the button to call emergency.

Cameron yelled loudly into her ear. "Peggy! Stay with me, Peggy! Help is on the way!"

Spying an empty bottle on the floor next to the bed, she knelt to read the label.

"What did she take?" Joshua asked.

"Benzodiazepines." She showed him the date on the label. "This bottle was filled yesterday morning."

# Chapter Seventeen

"Is it us?" Cameron asked Joshua while they watched Hancock County's sheriff, Curt Sawyer, talking to Peggy Lawson's neighbor. "Everywhere we go lately, mayhem breaks out."

Short and muscular, Curt Sawyer had never let go of his Marine training. One look from him intimidated anyone into saying and doing whatever he wanted. That was what made him a good sheriff.

Their ears were still ringing from the ambulance sirens that had whisked Peggy Lawson off to the hospital. It did not look good. She had never regained consciousness.

Looking distraught by the happenings next door only a few yards from her home, the neighbor was holding her young daughter with both hands on her shoulders. The girl clutched a long-haired black cat in her arms. The residents of the quiet neighborhood had suddenly woken up to emergency vehicles filling one of their yards.

"In the last twenty-four hours," Cameron noted, "we've had a hostage situation and shooting, arson and attempted murder, got nailed by your son for premarital sex, and now an attempted suicide."

"Just your average day in a small town," Joshua replied as Curt Sawyer crossed the driveway to join them.

"Well, so far, everything seems to be on the up and up for an attempted suicide." The sheriff pointed his pen in the direction of the mother leading her daughter into their home. "Mrs. Clark says Peggy Lawson gave her cat, Toby, to her daughter yesterday morning, without asking permission from her. Mrs. Clark didn't like that. So she kept coming over here to try to talk to Peggy about it. She says she was here knocking on the door about five times throughout the day and getting no answer. But she knew Peggy was home because her car was in the driveway. Then, last night, around ten o'clock, when she was getting ready to go to bed, she heard the car start up. She says she came running out in her bathrobe to try to catch her, but the car was speeding down the road and wouldn't stop. She heard the car come back in a little after eleven. By then, Mrs. Clark gave up and decided to let her daughter keep the cat."

Joshua said, "Getting her affairs in order. Giving away her cat to make sure it was well taken care of."

"But one last thing," Cameron said, "before she went, take out the man who she blamed for ruining her life."

Joshua opened the sedan's driver side door. A puzzled expression crossed his face.

"What's wrong?" she asked him. "Why are you giving me the face?"

"Did you see all the booze stacked up on that kitchen counter?" Joshua asked them.

"She was inebriated," Curt said. "Liquid courage."

"As much booze as she had in her, she drove over to Hookstown and set fire to a house with gasoline and matches, but she didn't set herself on fire." Joshua turned to Cameron. "Did you smell gasoline while trying to revive her?"

"No." Startled, Cameron shook her head. "But I did smell vomit and body odor, which means she didn't shower."

"As drunk as she was, she would have smelled like gasoline." Joshua studied the driver's seat in the car. "How tall would you say Peggy Lawson is?"

"Five feet-eight inches easy." She looked over his shoulder at the front seat of the sedan. It was pushed up all the way to the steering wheel.

"Whoever last drove this car was short."

Cameron knelt next to the car to examine the tires.

Joshua shook his head. "I don't know what to tell you about the car and the arson, but I can tell you this, my gut is telling me that Peggy didn't drive this car last. I think she spent the whole day locked up inside drinking up courage to take a bottle of pills."

"Josh, come take a look," Cameron called, "and tell me what you find in the treads of this tire."

After kneeling next to her, Joshua studied the front tire. He sniffed at what appeared to be mud embedded in the tread. Not satisfied, he rubbed his gloved finger over it and held it up to his nose to smell. "Horse manure."

"*Horse* manure. How do you know it's not *cow* manure?" Curt asked.

"Cow manure has a distinctive smell and consistency," Joshua replied. "This is *horse* manure."

Cameron turned to the sheriff. "And Doris Sullivan breeds and trains Thoroughbred horses."

Joshua slowly rose to his feet. "Forensics can extract the DNA from this manure and, if they can get samples from the horses on Doris' farm, trace it back to the horse that left it, which would place this car at her farm if there's a match." He told Curt, "We need to impound this car, and have forensics go over it with a fine tooth comb. Whoever set that fire tried to frame Peggy for doing it."

❧ ❧ ❧ ❧

"I never said I *didn't* have a second freezer," Doris insisted from her hospital bed.

"But you did deliberately mislead us by not mentioning that you owned a second freezer," Joshua said.

"Which is now in the barn." With a pained expression, she sat up to look down the length of the bed at where Cameron stood on the other side of Joshua. "I take it that it's still there in the feed room."

"Yes, it is," Cameron said. "We're talking about the *other* freezer—the one that was there before this one."

"The one you tried to blow up in Albert's house to keep from being discovered," Joshua explained.

"You know," Cameron said, "the one that had Cheryl Smith's body in it."

Doris pursed her lips together so tight that her mouth resembled a beak. "I have no idea what you're talking about. Now, leave. In case you didn't notice someone tried to kill me last night." She sat up. "I'm the victim here, and you're accusing me of murder."

Joshua placed a hand on Cameron's and softened his tone. "I'm sorry, Doris. We're simply trying to figure all this out. Someone did try to kill you last night, and someone also killed your daughter. We need to know the truth if we're to determine if the two things are connected."

"Angie was not—" Tears came to Doris' eyes. She sniffed.

Never comfortable with sobbing victims, witnesses, or suspects, Cameron stepped away from the bed. It was additionally disconcerting for her since Doris had come across as so tough. Tears in her eyes did not appear right. They didn't look like they belonged there.

Joshua took a box of tissue from the bedside table and handed a tissue to the elderly woman. "Who knew about you and Ralph?"

"No one," she replied. "Ralph and I have a complicated relationship. The last time he and I were together was before Peggy came along. That was *years* ago." She sucked in a deep breath. When she spoke again, her voice grew stronger. "It used to be just sex between him and me. But then, after Angie died, we became friends … who had sex. No strings. It's nice to have a companion like that. Then he took up with Peggy, and we became friends without sex. This weekend, after he broke it off with her, he came over and … Well, you know."

"Did Mildred know?" Joshua asked.

"If she did, I didn't tell her."

"But you did tell her that Ralph had left her," he reminded her.

"I was messing with her," Doris said. "I've been messing with her for decades. It's what we do. If Mildred doesn't know what Ralph is, she's deaf, dumb, and blind." She chuckled. "I knew it the second I laid eyes on him."

"If you know what he is, why do you put up with him?" Cameron asked.

Doris ticked off the points on her fingers. "He doesn't tell me what to do, he doesn't ask anything of me, and he's damn good in bed." She puffed out her chest and nodded her head. "You can't ask for a better man than that."

"There's someone for everyone," Joshua said.

Cameron stepped in. "Tell us about the freezer and you blowing up the house."

Doris pointed a bony finger at her. "You can't prove I blew up the house."

"But you knew the freezer was down there," Joshua said. "That's why you blew it up. You didn't want us to find the body."

"It had your fingerprints and traces of horse feed in it," the detective said. "That's enough for us to take you in."

"I'm an old woman," Doris said in a mocking tone.

"Old women get convicted of murder all the time," Cameron said.

Joshua again put his hand on Cameron's. With his eyes, he told her that he would handle this questioning. Stepping back, she held her hands up in surrender.

He turned to Doris. "I'm trying to help you. I can't if you don't start telling me the truth. It is your freezer. Cheryl Smith's body was found in it. Cheryl was a prime suspect in the murder of your daughter. That gives you a very strong motive for killing her. Cameron's right. She has enough to arrest you for murder. I don't want that to happen. I want to help you. So fill in the blanks. Tell us where she's wrong."

Doris stuck out her chin. Her nose was up in the air when she said, "Because you'd never believe the truth."

"Try me."

"Okay." She paused to look from Joshua to Cameron and then back to him before saying, "Someone stole it."

Cameron and Joshua exchanged glances before they both turned back to the old woman in the bed.

"Someone stole your freezer and put a dead body in it and hid it in your neighbor's basement?" Cameron asked.

"I told you that you wouldn't believe me."

"You mean to tell me that you walked into the barn one morning and—" said Joshua.

"Found it missing," Doris said. "All the feed was taken out of it and sitting in a pile in the feed room. There were tire tracks leading up to and into the barn."

"Did you ever report it?" Cameron asked.

"Are you kidding? It was an old, broken-down freezer. I used it to store the horse feed in to keep the mice and raccoons out. It had no monetary value. I just bought an old freezer from a garage sale and used that."

"Do you recall when this happened?" asked Joshua.

"Right after all that stink with Mildred about that freezer I had donated to the yard sale," Doris said. "I remember because I half-suspected that it was Mildred who stole it, but then I remembered that it didn't work. If she was going to steal my freezer, she would have stolen one that worked."

"That would put it in the summer of 1985," Joshua said.

"Yes, that would be it." Doris gestured with a wave of her hand. "I had forgotten all about it until you gave me a tour of Albert's house to see what had to be done to get it cleaned out so that I could buy his farm. When you took me down to the basement and I saw my freezer, I about had a stroke. I recognized it because of a dent in the front from where a horse had broken out of his stall and gotten into the feed room and kicked it. I couldn't for the life of me figure out why Albert had stolen my freezer. Later, I came back. I remembered I had a key that Albert had given me eons ago. So I went to look inside to see why he had stolen it—" Her eyes grew wide at the memory. "I didn't even recognize her as Cheryl Smith. Albert was my friend. I meant it when I said I had forgiven him for helping Cheryl get permission to leave town after killing Angie. When I saw that dead body, all I wanted to do was help cover it up so people wouldn't be saying all sorts of cruel things about him. I figured that if he was a killer or sex fiend, then he would already be getting his judgment and punishment up in heaven. I wasn't thinking about any of this tracing back to me. I was trying to protect Albert, not me, when I made that bomb."

"But there were a dozen people in that house," Joshua said.

"That's why I came upstairs to get you," Doris said. "I'd set the timer to give you enough time to get everyone out. When you weren't there, I took her down," she pointed at Cameron, "and let her put out the call to clear the house."

Joshua opened his mouth to argue, but Cameron cut him off. "Let me get this straight. You went out to the barn one morning and found that your broken down freezer had been hauled away in the middle of the night. Then, almost thirty years later, it turns up in your neighbor's basement with the dead body of the woman accused of killing your daughter. So then you built a bomb and tried to blow up the house to protect said neighbor's reputation without knowing anything about who stole the freezer, who killed your daughter's suspected killer, and who hid your freezer containing the dead body of your daughter's suspected killer in your neighbor's basement."

"That's right," Doris smirked.

"I believe her," Cameron told Joshua.

"You also believe sugar-free ice cream has zero calories," he replied.

"Which is why I can eat as much as I want of it," Cameron said while answering the buzz on her hip from her cell phone.

Simultaneously, Joshua's cell phone vibrated to signal an incoming call. While Cameron read the text message on her phone, he was talking on his.

"Gail Hildebrand just texted. She and Ned want us to stop by the Mountaineer ASAP," Cameron told them.

"And the state attorney general suggests I call his people who are doing the audit at the Mountaineer. I guess they found something," Joshua said.

# Chapter Eighteen

"This is unbelievable!" In his corner office on the ground floor of the Mountaineer, Ned Carter was pacing and cursing while Gail Hildebrand pleaded for him to calm down. He stopped and whirled around at the two investigators who had traveled up from Charleston, West Virginia, to audit the casino's books. "*I* called *you!* Why would I call you to come up here and investigate my business if I was stealing from it myself?"

The shorter of the two men shrugged. "Maybe because you sensed the jig was up."

Meanwhile, the taller and older investigator chewed on a toothpick while leaning with his back against the wall.

When Cameron and Joshua came in, Gail rushed to them. "You have to do something. They're accusing Ned of embezzlement. He didn't do it. Tell them he didn't do it."

"He didn't do it," Cameron said.

"Exactly who are you?" The shorter investigator took a step toward Cameron only to collide with Joshua's arm that shot out to block him.

"She's with me." Joshua looked down into his eyes.

"And you are?"

"Joshua Thornton, Hancock County prosecuting attorney. Your boss suggested I come over to find out what was going on."

The investigator glared at Ned. "I don't care who your friends are. You've been stealing money from your investors, and I intended to make you pay for it."

"Exactly what evidence do you have that he's been doing that," Cameron asked.

"Our people have been monitoring the resort's accounting system for some time," the investigator said. "We knew the cocky bastard would make his move eventually. Sure enough, last night he did. At ten-fifty-four, he logged into the accounts remotely and transferred two hundred-thousand dollars out of the retirement funds to an off-shore account."

"Have you been able to track who owns that account?" Joshua asked.

The older investigator removed the toothpick from his mouth. "The money trail disappeared after that. We were only able to follow it so far. Our forensics people have gone back over ten years, and they are still collecting evidence. It started out as a very small amount. A normal audit would barely notice it. Then, over the years, it has increased with time until now it is almost blatant—especially in the last month. It's like he's taunting us."

The shorter investigator pointed in Ned's direction. "And the trail keeps leading back to you and your wife."

Gail turned to Cameron. "I told you she'd pull something like this."

"She?" the shorter investigator laughed. "I doubt it. She's his accomplice. We have information that the money he's been stealing he's used to build his wife's winery."

Cameron's eyes narrowed. "Exactly what kind of information."

The investigator's mouth clamped shut.

"Was this an anonymous informant by any chance?" she asked.

"Have you found the money in the winery's accounts?" Joshua asked them.

Both of the state investigators fell silent.

With a glance at his young partner, the taller one shook his head. "This informant has only started contacting us in the last couple of weeks. We haven't finished investigating his lead yet."

"Ned is being framed," Gail said. "Can't you see that?"

Slowly, the older investigator nodded his head. "Personally, I think our culprit is too slick. The way he's been skimming from the accounts—I think if the trail is pointing to Ned Carter—then we need to go in another direction."

The younger partner's eyes bulged. His mouth grew tight.

"I told you to let us finish the investigation before you go hurling accusations," the older man told his partner.

To the others, he said, "You have to excuse Higgins. He's young and a little trigger happy. He's still got some learning to do."

"Don't they all?" Joshua replied.

With a congenial tone, the older investigator assured Ned,"We'll be keeping you informed about our investigation. If you think of anything, tell us. In the meantime, keep our investigation hush-hush. Hopefully, our guy will make a mistake, and we can catch him." With a nod of his head, he tapped the younger man on the shoulder and gestured for the door.

"But—" Higgins objected.

"We're leaving."

"How—"

"I said we're leaving, Higgins," the older man ordered. "Go! We'll talk about it in the car." Like a father leading out a misbehaving son, he stuck the toothpick back into his mouth and pointed toward the door.

Gail rushed to throw her arms around Ned, who sighed with relief. She turned to Cameron and Joshua. "Thank you."

"Don't thank us," Joshua said. "Thank the big guy with the toothpick.

"That was Investigator Frost," Ned said. "I think those were the most words he's said in one sitting since they came to town a couple of months ago. I never thought he was on our side before."

"I didn't even know he was the boss," Gail said.

"I guess he's the strong, silent type." Cameron sat down in the chair across from Ned's desk. "Any idea who the embezzler is?"

"I thought it was Brianne," Gail said, "but she'd never throw suspicion on herself by putting the money in her own account like that."

With a thoughtful look in his eyes, Ned said, "She is computer savvy."

"How savvy?" Cameron said. "The way investigator Frost is talking, our perp is very good at covering his tracks. Very good. Not only is he skimming money from the Mountaineer, but he's doing it under your accounts so that if it was picked up, everyone would think it was you."

"But he's not hiding it so much anymore," Joshua said. "Now he's turned informant and is pointing the finger at both Ned and Brianne."

"After years. What brought that on?" Cameron looked over her shoulder at Joshua who was standing behind her. "It kind of reminds me of some serial killers, who are so good that no one notices that there is a serial killer out there. Infuriated that no one notices how good they are, they step up the game to get the recognition they feel they deserve. That's usually when they get caught."

"If this has been going on for over ten years, then we know the guy isn't sloppy," Joshua said.

"That means he's cocky."

"Can you think of anyone with a grudge against you," Joshua asked Ned. "Someone who also has the technical knowledge to pull this off?"

Ned shook his head before turning to Gail. Together, the two of them stared at each other while deep in thought.

Cameron was struck by how the two of them played off each other the same way she believed she and Joshua did. Sometimes, she felt as if Joshua could read her thoughts. It was not unusual for one of them to finish the other's sentence. *I can't see Brianne being into anyone enough to finish his sentence.*

As if he were reading her mind, Joshua stepped up behind her chair and put his hands on her shoulders. She reached up to touch is fingers. Recalling his touch the night before, she felt a wave of emotion sweep over her.

Gail interrupted the silence. "Kyle … but that was so long ago."

"This started so long ago," Joshua reminded her.

"Kyle, as in Kyle Bostwick?" Cameron asked.

Ned chuckled at Gail. "Now, you're reaching."

She ticked off on her fingers. "You two had a big falling out—"

"Over what?" Joshua asked.

"Kyle was the contractor that set up the computer network for the Mountaineer," Ned said. "I set up the contract when I first became manager. We were his biggest account. We put his company on the map. But then, the board decided Kyle's company was too small to handle such a big operation. They voted to employ an in-house staff to take care of our IT needs. The next time the contract came up, we didn't renew." He shook his head. "That was over fifteen years ago."

"Which was when your friendship ended," Gail said.

"But I thought Kyle set up the network for the winery," Cameron said.

"Friends with Brianne, not with me," Ned said. "In case, you haven't noticed, Brianne and I lead separate lives."

Gail told them, "Kyle knows everything about computers, programs—everything."

"He did set up our complete system," Ned said.

"Which means he'd know how to hack into your accounting system," Gail said. "He's also got a huge ego. Every time I see him, I swear he's smirking at me because he feels so superior."

"He's got an ego," Cameron said.

"And a big grudge." Gail turned to Ned. "Tell her what Kyle said when you two had that fight after he found out about the contract."

"What did he tell me?" Ned asked.

"About Angie," she reminded him.

Joshua stood up straight. "What about Angie?"

Ned's cheeks turned pink. "I forgot about that."

"How could you?" Gail asked.

"Because I wanted to."

"What did Kyle say?" Cameron asked.

Gail nudged Ned with her elbow. After a deep sigh, he told them, "Kyle called me a traitor. He said it was my fault that Angie was dead. If anyone deserved to die at the bottom of that river, it was me and Brianne … and Angie's Mom because it was our fault Cheryl killed her."

Cameron exchanged glances with Joshua. "Did you see Cheryl when she came to town?"

"I already told you, no," Ned replied.

"Did she call you?"

"No."

"Did you know she had come back to town?" Cameron asked him.

Ned hesitated before nodding. "Kyle called me. He said Cheryl had come into the winery looking for Brianne … and me. She wanted to hook up with me. I told him I didn't want to see her …" His voice trailed off.

"What else?" Joshua prodded him. "What else did Kyle say?"

"I was surprised when he wanted me to see her. Out of anyone, I thought for sure he would want no one to help her in any way. But he said that maybe I should. I told him, one, I was not in the business anymore." Ned went on to explain, "I got out of dealing when I graduated from college. I was never big time. I only dealt with my friends. Two, I had no desire to see her. As a matter of fact, I told Kyle that if I did see her that I'd call the police. That was when Kyle suggested that I do see her, and help her out with a fix—that would kill her." He swallowed. "Kyle wanted me to murder her."

"With a drug overdose," Cameron whispered.

"I couldn't believe what I was hearing. Kyle, of all people. I thought he was a wuss."

"What did you say?" Joshua asked.

"No," Ned said. "And I told him that I was going to forget we had this conversation and pretend it never happened. Such was the case until I didn't renew our contract. Then he brought it up again and said I was a traitor because I refused to kill Cheryl after what she had done to Angie."

"Did you give him the drugs to kill Cheryl?" Cameron asked him.

Ned sighed and exchanged glances with Gail, who nodded for him to answer. "I gave him the name of a guy I knew who dealt."

Cameron stood up and Joshua took her hand. With a glance over her shoulder, she told them that they had been very helpful and left.

Out in the corridor, she told Joshua, "Next stop,—"

"—Kyle Bostwick's home."

# CHAPTER NINETEEN

Kyle Bostwick's home was a modest one story on the corner block of Indiana Avenue and Fourth Street. It was an older house with a tiny fenced-in back yard. Kyle was notorious amongst his neighbors for being less than friendly if any four-legged neighbors managed to get onto his property.

His face and tone was devoid of pleasantry when he opened the door to find Cameron and Joshua on his porch. "Detective Gates, still chasing your tail I see."

"If you're referring to going around in circles, yes," Cameron replied. "Can we come in?"

Kyle paused to look her up and down, and then caught Joshua's eye before stepping back to let them inside.

As they stepped into the living room, Cameron and Joshua were first struck by the array of pictures, almost like a montage, of Angie Sullivan on almost every surface and wall. On every wall and shelf, there were pictures of Angie from seemingly every stage of her life.

"How many pictures do you have of me in your house?" Cameron whispered to Joshua.

"None," he replied. "How many do you have of me?"

"None. Are we strange?"

"Angie was the love of my life," Kyle scoffed when he overheard them. "Of course, I'd have pictures of her. Just because she's dead doesn't mean I've forgotten her. I guess you wouldn't understand that. Few people nowadays understand the concept of loyalty."

"Kyle, we know what happened to Cheryl Smith," Joshua said.

The corners of his lips curled into a grin that resembled that of the Joker in the Batman movies. "Really?"

"You were the only one to see her when she came back to town," Joshua said.

"No, I didn't."

Cameron countered, "Brianne Davenport says you told her that Cheryl came by the winery to sell her Ferrari. You gave her Brianne's business card. The front had Brianne's phone number to set up selling her the car. The back had Ned's phone number for her to call him to arrange a hook up for drugs and sex."

Kyle laughed. "Who do you think the jury is going to believe? Brianne, who's had Cherry Pickens' Ferrari in her garage all these years, and who built her business using money that her husband has skimmed from the Mountaineer's profits. Or Ned Carter, who dealt in heroin and whose phone number was found in Cherry's pocket. And—Oh, what about the freezer that Cheryl's body was found in? Have you found out yet who that belonged to?"

Seeing Joshua's glare, Kyle chuckled. "I guess you did." He folded his arms over his thin chest. "Now, what do you have against me?"" At a loss of any real evidence against him, Kyle waved his hands like a magician who has committed an outstanding trick.

"Your DNA," Cameron answered.

Kyle's beady eyes, magnified by his glasses, widened.

"I guess Cheryl gets horny when she gets high," Cameron said. "She had sex shortly before her neck was snapped. Since you gave her the heroin, I guess that means you were there. You figured what the heck, and had sex with her. Then you killed her." With a chuckle, she held up her finger. "Your mistake was sealing her in that freezer, which was airtight, which kept your semen viable all these years."

"Considering that we have witnesses who said you saw Cheryl when she was here, I can assure you Detective Gates won't have any problem getting a warrant for your DNA to compare to the semen they found in Cheryl Smith's body," Joshua said.

Tears seeped out of Kyle's eyes to roll down his cheeks.

"Seven years is a long time to think about something," Cameron said. "If you think about it long and hard enough, and replay it in your mind over and over again, facts and circumstances have a way of working their way to the surface. Some can become twisted. By the time Cheryl walked into the winery that day, you had come to blame not only her for Angie's murder, but her friends and mother for the roles they played in it happening."

"First, you blamed Cheryl for breaking you and Angie up." She cocked her head at him. "Then, there was Brianne, who told Cheryl about Doris being her mother. You also tracked down who had planted the seed in Cheryl's mind about Angie having an affair with Ned behind her back."

"I suppose you blamed Ned for letting it happen," Joshua said, "and Doris for being the source of the family secret that hurt the woman you loved."

"So you decided to kill Cheryl for revenge and frame each one of them," Cameron said.

"You gave Cheryl the business card with Brianne's private number on the front and Ned's phone number on the back," Joshua said. "Then, you arranged a meeting where she would pick up some drugs from Ned. Only you showed up instead with heroin that you got from a source he had given you."

Cameron said, "He told us that you wanted him to kill her, but he refused."

Kyle's eyes narrowed. Behind the glasses, they looked like dark slits.

"That left you to do it by yourself," she said. "Why did you break her neck? Why didn't you just let her OD?"

"Because I don't know anything about drugs," he muttered. "She passed out, but she wouldn't die. I didn't know if she would wake up or not. I waited for so long but she kept breathing. Finally, I got tired of waiting and snapped her neck with a shovel." Kyle's glare hardened as he stared at the montage on the wall behind them.

Joshua picked up the story. "You still had to implicate Doris. So you stole the freezer from her barn and hid it in the basement of Albert Gordon's house."

"He was Cheryl Smith's lawyer," Kyle said. "He let her get away."

"Then you left the Ferrari on Brianne's doorstep to complete the frame," Cameron said. "Then you just waited for her body to be found. Betcha you never thought it would be twenty-eight years."

"I'll bet that's why you pushed the envelope in embezzling funds from the Mountaineer," Joshua said. "You got tired of waiting for Ned and Brianne to get theirs for setting up Angie."

"Those stupid auditors were taking forever to find the money trail leading to the winery."

"Which is why you stepped up the game by turning anonymous informant," Joshua said. "Why now?

"Running out of time," Kyle said. "Couldn't wait any longer for them to get theirs." He chuckled, "Brianne is so clueless. She actually believes all the money in her accounts is profits from the winery."

"You've been robbing Peter to pay Paul to frame them both," Cameron said.

"Never once has so much as a penny landed in any of my accounts," Kyle said. "So none of you can prove any of it."

"Do you want to bet?" Cameron said. "We will get your DNA to prove you were with Cheryl when she came to town. Ned gave us the name of the drug dealer that you bought the heroin from. We'll get a search warrant for your gardening shed and find that shovel you used."

"The forensics auditor will prove that your computer was used for the embezzling," Joshua said. "It may take time, but once we tell them who did it, they will find your trail."

"You're coming with us." Cameron removed her handcuffs from their case in her utility belt. She gestured for him to turn around.

Not moving or saying anything, Kyle looked from her to Joshua and back to her again. He turned around to look at the various pictures spread throughout the living room. "I need to call my lawyer," he said after a long silence.

"You can do that at the department," Cameron gestured again. "Put your hands on top of your head and turn around."

As she stepped toward him, he shoved her with both hands in the chest. She fell back against Joshua who caught her in his arms. While they both managed to stay on their feet, the split second that they were caught off guard was long enough for Kyle to run down the short hallway to the master bedroom and slam the door. He had already locked it by the time they reached it.

"Call for backup," Joshua ordered. "We have a barricade situation."

Cameron had her radio to her ear. "What do you think I'm doing?" Into the radio, she said, "Officer needs assistance, we have a—"

Her call for backup was cut off by the sound of a single gunshot from inside the bedroom.

Stunned, Cameron stared at Joshua. His eyes were as big as she felt hers were.

The house screamed with silence.

The operator on the other end of the radio called out for a response from Cameron. "Detective Gates? Are you able to respond?"

"We need to go in," Joshua said.

"Break the door down."

Clutching her gun, Cameron stepped back while Joshua kicked in the bedroom door. The first thing to hit them as the door burst open was the smell of the gunshot residue.

Inside, they found the bedroom to be as immaculate as the rest of the house. The queen-sized bed was encased in white sheets. Nothing was out of order. In the corner of the bedroom they found a shrine erected out of a vanity filled with lit candles in honor of Angelina Sullivan. Her pictures surrounded the blood-splattered mirror.

At the foot of Angelina Sullivan's shrine rested the body of the man who loved her in both life and death: Kyle Bostwick, who took his life with a bullet through his temple.

# CHAPTER TWENTY

"Two suicides in Chester in one twenty-four hour period." Sheriff Curt Sawyer plopped down in a chair he had pulled up to the end of Joshua and Cameron's booth.

"One suicide," Joshua corrected him. "Tad says Peggy is going to survive. But it was a close one."

"And all over love," Cameron said. "I'd never kill myself over a man."

"Not even me?" Joshua asked.

"Not even you," she replied. "I'm still young and reasonably pretty. I'd find someone else."

"What makes it a challenge is finding someone who would not only put up with you, but share his ice cream with you."

They sat back to allow the server to deliver their special sundae, along with two spoons. She handed them both to Joshua, who gallantly handed one to Cameron. When she reached to take it, he grasped her hand and kissed it.

"You two can be so sickening," Curt groaned. "To change the topic to something that is less upsetting to my stomach, who offed Angie Sullivan and then tried to kill her mother?

Was it Kyle? He did have this delusional fantasy about their love."

"According to Ned and Brianne, Kyle's story got bigger over time," Cameron said "Brianne did say that Angie didn't feel like dealing with ending it that night. I think he became delusional after she died."

"How about the arson at Doris' house?" Curt asked.

"Kyle had an alibi." Joshua shook his head. "He was on the computer embezzling money from the Mountaineer in Ned's name, and then transferring it to an offshore account before depositing it into account that has Brianne's name—"

"Would you believe all that money he was stealing and moving around, he'd never touch himself?" Cameron smiled. "He was a man of ethics."

"A sick man of ethics," Curt said.

"In more ways than one," Joshua said with a somber expression and tone. He looked up at Cameron. "Do you remember Kyle's comment about him running out of time. That was why he became so bold in the last month or so with the embezzling and even called the investigators to implicate Ned and Brianne."

"Yes," she replied. "What did he mean by that?"

"He was dying," Joshua said.

Stunned, Curt and Cameron both sat back in their seats.

"Advance stages of prostate cancer," Joshua said. "Tad found it during the autopsy. He wanted to see justice for Angie by getting revenge on all those who hurt her before he died."

"Wow," Cameron breathed. "That would make you think he did try to kill Doris, but he had an airtight alibi."

Curt shook his head. "It wasn't Peggy who tried to burn out Ralph and Doris—"

"That's one of the things we need to figure out," she said. "Who was the intended victim? Ralph or Doris?"

"Or both?" Joshua said while answering his phone.

"Doris says no one knows about her and Ralph," Cameron said.

When Joshua held up his finger to indicate that he was listening to the person on the other end of the phone, she turned to Curt. "The intimate part of their relationship has been off for years."

One of Curt's bushy eyebrows arched. "She says."

"Thanks, Tad. That's a help." Joshua disconnected the call and placed the phone on top of the table. "Tad finally got a report back from the state medical examiner about her exam of Angie Sullivan's body."

"Did they find anything helpful after all these years of being buried underground?" Curt asked.

"As a matter of fact, he did," Joshua said. "It wasn't just one blow to the back of her skull, like the original report said. It was two. One was right on top of the other, so what was mistaken as cracks from one blow, was actually, with a closer x-ray, two blows that were almost right on top of each other. Plus, there was a fracture to the temple that he thinks was a blow with the same type of weapon."

Cameron visualized. "She was hit first, most likely from the front—"

"Facing her killer," Joshua said.

"Knocking her down," she said. "Then, while she's down, she's hit two more times."

"The state medical examiner thinks it was a tire iron." Joshua put down his spoon and rubbed his hands. "Something else, the medical examiner found. Angie had a dislocated shoulder. The cartilage was torn where her arm fit into her shoulder joint."

"What does that mean?" she asked.

"It indicates that she could have been dragged by her arms."

"Like to be put back into the car," Cameron said. "She was knocked out with a tire iron, and then put back into the car, and it was dumped in the river."

"Which Cheryl witnessed," Joshua said.

Deep in thought, Cameron had stopped eating. She scratched her head. "If Cheryl didn't do it—"

"How about Brianne?" Curt asked. "Cheryl was blackmailing the killer. Brianne had the bucks, and Cheryl did go to see her when she came into town."

Considering the thought, Cameron looked over at the sheriff.

Joshua caught her attention. "I can guarantee you, if Brianne did it, we'll need a trunk load of evidence to get her into court."

"According to what Kyle had said—" she mused.

"If you can believe him," Curt interjected.

"Let's say he was telling the truth about everything," she said. "Granted, Ned and Brianne claim Angie was planning to dump Kyle—"

"She did have the ring on her finger when we found her body," Joshua said.

"I don't think Kyle killed her." Cameron held up both of her hands to silence them. "He was convinced Cheryl did it. He even inserted Albert Gordon, Cheryl's lawyer in his revenge." She tapped the table top with her finger. "According to Kyle's statement, it was late at night when she dropped him off at his house. Even in 1978, a girl alone doesn't get out of the car in the dark and let someone get close enough to hit her with a tire iron."

"Unless it was someone she trusted," Joshua said.

"Like Brianne," Curt said.

Cameron said, "Do you still have Angie's car in the impound yard?"

"Angie Sullivan's murder is still a cold case." Curt nodded. "It's in the impound yard at Maple's Garage up at Hill Crest Ridge."

~ ~ ~ ~

"What's their names?" Cameron asked about the Rottweiler and white German shepherd standing guard inside the impound yard behind Maple's Garage.

The namesake for the garage was Mark Maple, a burly looking man in work jeans. He responded to the detective's question with a devilish smile. His bushy mustache twitched when he glanced over at Joshua, who seemed equally amused.

"I'm clearly the outsider of an inside joke," Cameron thought.

"The Rottweiler's name is Uno," Mark told her. "The German shepherd is Dallas."

"Do they bite?" she asked.

Both men broke out into laughter. "Uno will kill you if he wants to," Mark finally answered in a low voice.

Taking her by the arm, Joshua led the detective away from the gate leading into impound yard. "Mark will take Uno inside the garage, and then we can go inside."

Once the big dog was locked up, the garage owner threw open the gate to allow them inside. "I think its back in the corner over there." He pointed with a wrench to the far corner of the yard. "It's a white Toyota sedan. By now it'll be rust colored."

He waited until they were several yards in and had stepped into the tall overgrown brush before calling out, "Watch out for snakes!"

Shrieking, Cameron almost jumped into Joshua's arms. With wicked laugh, Mark went back inside the garage.

Like a canine tour guide, Dallas escorted them through the rows upon rows of crashed vehicles of every size, shape, and age. Many of the cars were victims of accidents. Others vehicles had taken part in crimes, which made them evidence. Until their cases were solved, they would remain locked up in the impound yard, with Uno and Dallas to guard them.

As they neared the further corner, the tall grass came up almost to their hips.

Joshua spotted the car first. Mark had been correct. It was a pile of rust.

"If there's any evidence here, I doubt if it's still good," Cameron said while trying to peer through the windows caked with decades' worth of dirt.

Joshua shook the keys out of the evidence envelope into his gloved palm. "The car has been locked up all this time. No one has been inside since it was originally examined."

"Back in 1984." Studying each part of it, up and down, she walked around the car. *What kind of evidence would still be on this puppy to prove who killed Angie Sullivan in the prime of her life?*

Joshua met her at the rear end of the car to hand her the keys. As he was handing them to her, he stopped. She reached out to touch the keys when she noticed him staring at the rear of the sedan. She turned her head to follow his eyes to the rear bumper, which was smashed into the trunk. "Could that have happened when it was pushed into the river?" she asked him.

He shook his head. "It was found nose first in the river."

She knelt down to study the bumper. "Is it possible that whoever pushed her in used their own car to do it?" The streaks of blue paint appeared to leap out at her.

She turned to grin up at Joshua. "We've got her."

# Chapter Twenty-One

"Of course, I was devastated to learn that my husband was cheating on me," Mildred Hildebrand said to the group of friends sitting around her kitchen table, "but I believe as a Christian woman, and a leader in our church, that it is my duty to set a good example by forgiving him." She patted her eyes with a lace handkerchief.

The woman dressed in purple reached over to pat her hand.

Mildred sucked in a deep breath. "You know, I wouldn't be one bit surprised if it came out that Doris Sullivan seduced him. She has never stopped chasing him, even after he married me. As soon as she found out that he had come to his senses and ended it with Peggy, she went chasing after him and dragged him back to her place."

One of the women was doubtful. "Dragged?" she asked with an arched eyebrow.

"Everyone knows how weak Ralph is." Mildred sighed and took a sip of her tea. "It's only because of my strength that our family has turned out so well."

"Mother," Gail's voice snapped when she came in with Joshua, Cameron, and Sheriff Curt Sawyer behind her. "Some people are here to see you."

Seeing the visitors, Mildred's eyes widened. "What has Ralph done now?"

Gasps were uttered from around the kitchen table.

"May we speak to you in the other room?" Joshua asked in a steady voice.

"Is Ralph okay?" the woman in purple asked.

"Ralph is fine," Curt answered. "He's waiting for us in the living room." He gestured at Mildred. "Can you please join us?"

Gail turned to the ladies. "I think it's best if you all go home now."

With questioning glances to each other, the three ladies got up and slowly made their way out the door. They all stopped in the foyer to peer into the living room where Ralph was waiting on the sofa. After shooting him shameful glances, they left.

Once they were gone, Mildred marched into the room and up to her husband. "Ralph, what have you done now?"

"Nothing," Ralph said. "I swear. I haven't even gone to the hospital to see Doris."

"And you have better not." Mildred wagged a finger at him. "I have friends at that hospital. If I so much as—"

"Mrs. Hildebrand, sit down," Cameron ordered.

"Mom, do what she says."

Mildred turned to the detective. "You can't come into my home and tell me—"

"Sit down!" Joshua snapped.

Mildred plopped down onto the sofa next to Ralph.

"Your reputation is very important to you, isn't it, Mrs. Hildebrand?" Joshua strolled around the living room, which contained a wide assortment of family pictures and a trophy case filled with certificates and awards.

"You are your reputation," she said. "Isn't your reputation important to you, Joshua?"

"Yes, I admit it is," he said. "But I also believe that who I am inside, who I see myself as being is more important than what others think of me."

Mildred cocked her head at him. "What are you trying to tell me, Joshua?" She gasped. "You're not giving me the elder position." She jumped up and whirled around at Ralph. "This is all your fault, you bastard! Because of your sneaking around!" She slapped him. "Look at what you've done to me!" She slapped him repeatedly until Curt and Joshua pulled her off him. "I'll kill you for this, Ralph! I'll kill you! You've ruined this family for the last time with your whoring around!"

The sheriff was surprised to discover that the older, heavyset woman was rather strong. Intent on finishing off her husband, she fought against them with everything she had, which included a knee to Curt's groin with such force that he buckled down to his knees.

"Are you okay?" Gail knelt to ask him.

Curt sucked in a breath. Unable to speak, he only nodded his head.

With his arms around her waist, Joshua dragged Mildred, still kicking and screaming, across the room and shoved her down into the recliner. "This is not about the elder position at the church!" he yelled at her. "Hell! I haven't even thought about it in over a week!" Catching himself swearing, he covered his mouth while Cameron smiled. "I'm talking about Angie Sullivan."

Mildred's face grew pale. She cleared her throat. "Doris' sister?"

"Mom, you know damn well that she was Doris' daughter and Dad was her father." Tears in her eyes, Gail shook her head. "What's wrong with you?"

With a groan, Curt slowly stood up.

"Even I felt that," Cameron whispered.

"Mildred, what did you do?" Ralph hissed at his wife from across the room.

"Shut up, Ralph," Mildred ordered. "Just shut your mouth."

"I think Ralph has plenty of right to speak," Joshua said, "considering that you tried to kill him and Doris Sullivan the other night."

"Mom," Gail wailed, "how could you?" Tears spilled from her eyes and down her cheeks.

"The first lesson in attempted murder is to wear gloves. Don't you ever watch television, Mrs. Hildebrand?" Cameron asked.

Mildred's face turned red. "I did wear gloves."

"When you drove Peggy Lawson's car," the detective said. "Not when you filled up the gas cans. Your fingerprints are all over them."

"You tried to kill me?" Ralph yelled. "Mildred, why? Why did you try to kill me?"

"Because you're a cheating son of a bitch, that's why!"

"But I always come back," he said.

"Maybe that's why she wanted you dead," Cameron said. "Did you ever think of that, Ralph?"

The old man looked confused.

"Appearances are very important to you, aren't they, Mildred?" Joshua asked. "Your status as an older church lady? A leader among your friends? That's why you killed Angie Sullivan. You were afraid that if Ralph left you for the mother of his child, that you would lose your status as a bigwig in this little town." He cocked his head at her. "Even worse, become an object of pity."

"I never knew Angie was Ralph's daughter," Mildred said. "I'd heard rumors. Hurtful rumors, most of them started by Doris."

"Doris wouldn't have done that," Cameron said. "It was a family secret. She never told anyone about it."

"I didn't even know," Ralph lied.

"You must have suspected," Joshua said. "Angie was so much younger than Doris. You know what type of man Ralph is. Then, when she started baring a resemblance to your children, your suspicions grew stronger. And then, Cheryl Smith started spreading the word."

"Suddenly, Angie Sullivan was a threat to you and the image that you had created in this little town," Cameron said. "She was reality personified."

"Angie was living proof of your husband's infidelity," Joshua said. "With her gone, you could continue living the lie that you had built."

"You can't prove any of that," Mildred said.

"In 1978, you drove a royal blue Cadillac," Cameron said.

"I always drive a royal blue Cadillac." Mildred smoothed the front of her skirt with her hands. "Every year, I buy the latest year's model."

"We know," Joshua said.

"As a matter of fact," Curt said, "back then, you were the only one in town who drove a 1978 royal blue caddie."

"It's what you used to push Angie's car into the river," Cameron said. "When you pushed it off the pier, you left your car's paint on hers. Forensics traced that paint back to the type of car you were driving back then."

Gail gasped. "I remember around the time Angie disappeared that your car's front end had been smashed. You said you hit a deer."

"Mildred," Ralph hissed. "Why? Angie was a sweet, sweet girl. She never did anything to you."

"Do you really think I didn't know that I was your second choice?" Mildred replied in a low angry voice. "You have always been in love with her mother."

Regaining her composure, Mildred looked up at Gail. "I'm not in denial. I've know the truth since day one. But I've always done what I needed to do to keep my family and my position as a leader in this community held in the highest regard." She smoothed her hair.

"Even if what needed to be done meant murder," Joshua said.

"You were out stalking Angie that night, weren't you?" Cameron said. "After she dropped Kyle off at his house, you got her to pull over off the road and slugged her with a tire iron."

Pleased with herself, Mildred smiled. "I waited until she had gotten out on Route 30 across the state line, where no one was around, and then I rear ended her—hard. I almost put her in a ditch. We pulled over, but she didn't want to get out of the car at first … until she saw it was me. Then she got out of the car all sweetness and light." She giggled. "She even called me Mrs. Hildebrand. She went back to look at the damage, and that was when I let her have it."

She frowned. "The hardest part was dragging her to get her back into the car. For a little girl, she was so heavy. I drove her car back to the yacht club. I parked it on the pier. And then I walked over to one of the bars and called a cab to take me back to my car. I started to tell him some story that I had made up about my daughter breaking down, but I saw he didn't care at all. He dropped me off at my car, and I drove back to the pier, put her car in neutral, and pushed it off the pier." She shrugged with a grin. "Within a few weeks, people stopped speculating about Ralph's illegitimate daughter, and my problem was gone. Everything went back to the way it was—the way it's supposed to be."

She looked around at the faces in the room. Gail's face was tear-soaked. Ralph's mouth was hanging open.

Shaking his head in disbelief, Curt Sawyer ordered Mildred to stand up. "Mildred Hildebrand, you're under arrest for the murder of Angelina Sullivan."

"We'll also be filing charges in Pennsylvania for arson and two counts of attempted murder," Cameron said.

"I was doing what I had to do to protect my family. It's the job of every matriarch. You understand that, don't you?" Mildred said.

"Actually, I don't," Cameron said.

# Epilogue

When Joshua offered to take Cameron anywhere she wanted for dinner that night, he was pleased, and not surprised, when she picked Cricksters. He wasn't disappointed, until they walked in for their date to find everyone they knew already there. Jan and Tad, Donny and his date, Kaden, who all happened to arrive at the same place for their Saturday night dates. The table was filled with food in various stages of being consumed. Tad and Jan were halfway through with their salads. Donny and Kaden were eating ice cream for a treat.

In spite of his efforts to tell Cameron that he wanted to be alone with her, Joshua discovered after ordering their sundae at the counter that she had pulled two chairs up to the table and joined the crowd.

Jan was still cringing about the news of who had killed sweet Angie Sulllivan. "Knowing Mildred all these years, I never would have known how insane she was."

"She was always a very proud woman, but I admit I never suspected she was capable of killing a young girl just to protect her own status and reputation," said Tad.

"Did Ralph Hildebrand have any idea about what his wife had done?" Donny asked.

"I doubt it," Cameron said.

"He doesn't play much of a role in any one's lives but his own," Joshua said.

"I feel sorry for Doris," Jan said. "She's been an innocent victim in all this. I guess she's out of the running for elder."

"Not so fast," Tad said. "Doris has gotten a lot of sympathy from many members of the board."

Joshua agreed. "It's all but official that she'll be taking Albert's place."

Donny and Jan exchanged grins.

"Ned Carter kicked Brianne to the curb. He's moved out of the Davenport mansion and in with Gail Hildebrand," said Cameron.

Jan smiled. "I'm glad. Gail really needs a shoulder to cry on right now. She deserves someone who loves her."

"I have to admit, I'm surprised," Joshua said. "I thought Ned was superficial, but when I saw him with Gail, I could see that he loved her."

"You can see that they have a connection," Cameron took Joshua's hand and flashed him a smile.

"Speaking of Brianne Davenport," Jan said, "what's happening in Hookstown, Pennsylvania, in regards to our prosecuting attorney shooting and killing Brianne's toy?"

"We had dinner with prosecutor Frank Ballister last night," Joshua told her.

"Oh," Jan said with a sarcastic laugh, "you had dinner with their prosecutor? I can see there's no old boy club stuff happening here."

"How many murder suspects have you had dinner with?" Tad asked Joshua.

"It wasn't murder," Joshua argued. "It was justifiable homicide. They had five witnesses to back up my statement. Tell them, Donny."

"Yeah, like he said," Donny replied with a wicked grin, which made Jan and Tad laugh even harder.

The clerk arrived with Joshua and Cameron's sundae built for two.

With the cock of an eyebrow in his father's direction, Donny glanced at his watch. "Look at the time, we have to go."

"Where are you going?" Cameron asked.

Casting a glance at his father, Donny stood up. "Kaden and I are meeting some friends."

"Really?" Kaden replied.

"Didn't I tell you?"

Joshua looked across the table at Tad. "Don't you and Jan have some place to go?"

Jan was puzzled. "Where's that?"

Catching Joshua's glare, Tad said, "Jan and I are going to the mall." He stood up. "We need to go pick out wallpaper for the nursery."

"We already picked out wallpaper." Jan glanced over at Joshua while Tad took her arm to pull her up to her feet.

Through the window, Cameron watched the two couples mingling out in the parking lot. "Was it something I said?"

"No." Joshua pointed at the sundae. "Eat up, and let's go home."

"Whose home?" she asked while scooping up the hot fudge. "Mine or yours?"

"I don't like you leaving me at the end of our dates."

"But you also don't like us sneaking around and hiding our sexual relationship from Donny."

"I hate it when you put it that way," Joshua said. "I don't think of us as having sex. You make us sound like a couple of animals. We're two people who happen to be in love, and we should be together."

She shot him a grin. "Are you saying you like having me around?"

The metal of the spoon made a clink sound when it hit metal at the bottom of the bowl. She looked up at him.

Joshua was smiling back at her.

With the spoon, she scooped up what he had concealed at the bottom of the bowl to reveal a diamond ring covered in hot fudge.

"When you find a woman who knows how to give a good back rub," he said, "you shouldn't let her get away."

With a smile, she licked off the hot fudge and placed the ring on her finger. She reached across the table to kiss him on the lips. When they parted, she gazed into his eyes. "It isn't every day you find a lover in crime."

After kissing him again, she held up the engagement ring to admire it on her finger. The edges of the round diamond were trimmed in chocolate fudge. She sighed. "I can't wait to tell Irving."

## The End

# About the Author

Lauren Carr fell in love with mysteries when her mother read Perry Mason to her at bedtime. The first installment in the Joshua Thornton mysteries, *A Small Case of Murder* was a finalist for the Independent Publisher Book Award. *A Reunion to Die For* was released in June 2007. Both of these books are in re-release.

The Mac Faraday Mysteries take place in Deep Creek Lake, Maryland. The first two books in her series, *It's Murder, My Son, Old Loves Die Hard,* and *Shades of Murder* have all been getting rave reviews from readers and reviewers.

This Lovers in Crime mystery, *Dead on Ice,* is Lauren's sixth mystery.

The owner of Acorn Book Services, Lauren is also a publishing manager, consultant, editor, cover and layout designer, and marketing agent for independent authors.

A popular speaker, Lauren has made appearances at schools, youth groups, and at conventions. She also passes on what she has learned in her years of writing and publishing by conducting workshops and seminars.

She lives with her husband, son, and two dogs on a mountain in Harpers Ferry, WV.

Visit Lauren's websites at:
Website: http://acornbookservices.com/
http://mysterylady.net/

CHECK OUT THESE OTHER HIGHLY-ACCLAIMED

# Lauren Carr Mysteries!

## The Mac Faraday Mysteries

## IT'S MURDER, MY SON

*An exciting mystery with plenty of intriguing and enigmatic characters, It's Murder, My Son is not a read that should be missed for mystery fans.*

**Reviewer: Margaret Lane, Midwest Book Reviews**

What started out as the worst day of Mac Faraday's life would end up being a new beginning. After a messy divorce hearing, the last person that Mac wanted to see was another lawyer. Yet, this lawyer wore the expression of a child bursting to tell his secret. This secret would reveal Mac as heir to undreamed of fortunes, and lead him to the birthplace of America's Queen of Mystery and an investigation that will unfold like one of her famous mystery novels.

Soon after she moves to her new lakefront home in Spencer, Maryland, multi-millionaire Katrina Singleton learns that life in an exclusive community is not all good. For some unknown reason, a strange man calling himself "Pay Back" begins stalking her. When Katrina is found strangled all evidence points to her terrorist, who is nowhere to be found.

Three months later, the file on her murder is still open with only vague speculations from the local police department when Mac Faraday, sole heir to his unknown birth mother's home and fortune, moves into the estate next door. Little does he know as he drives up to Spencer Manor that he is driving into a closed gate community that is hiding more suspicious deaths than his DC workload as a homicide detective. With the help of his late mother's journal, this retired cop puts all his detective skills to work to pick up where the local investigators have left off to follow the clues to Katrina's killer.

# Old Loves Die Hard

*The fast-paced complex plot brings surprising twists into a storyline that leads Mac and his friends into grave danger. Readers are drawn into Mac's past, meet his children, and experience the troubling relationships of his former in-laws. New fans will surely look forward to the next installment in this great new series.*

**Reviewer: Edie Dykeman**
**Bellaonline Mystery Books Editor**

Old Loves Die Hard…and in the worst places.

Retired homicide detective Mac Faraday, heir of the late mystery writer Robin Spencer, is settling nicely into his new life at Spencer Manor when his ex-wife Christine shows up—and she wants him back! Before Mac can send her packing, Christine and her estranged lover are murdered in Mac's private penthouse suite at the Spencer Inn, the five-star resort built by his ancestors.

The investigation leads to the discovery of cases files for some of Mac's murder cases in the room of the man responsible for destroying his marriage. Why would his ex-wife's lover come to Spencer to dig into Mac's old cases?

With the help of his new friends on Deep Creek Lake, Mac must use all of his detective skills to clear his name and the Spencer Inn's reputation, before its five-stars—and more bodies—start dropping!

## Shades of Murder

*Lauren Carr could give Agatha Christie a run for her money! This hypnotic page-turner is a whirlwind of romance, murder, and espionage. Lots of creativity went into the unforeseen twists, and culminated in a climactic ending that tied the multi-faceted story into a nice little package. I also appreciated the special attention paid to the animal characters, which were every bit as developed as their human counterparts. This was an absolutely delightful read that is sure to be a hit with mystery readers. I look forward to reading her other books, as I am now a fan!*

**Reviewer: Charlene Mabie-Gamble, Literary R&R**

In *Shades of Murder*, Mac Faraday is once again the heir to an unbelievable fortune. This time the benefactor is a stolen art collector. But this isn't just any stolen work-of-art—it's a masterpiece with a murder attached to it.

Ilysa Ramsay was in the midst of taking the art world by storm. Hours after unveiling her latest masterpiece—she is found dead in her Deep Creek Lake studio—and her painting is nowhere to be found. Almost a decade later, the long lost Ilysa Ramsay masterpiece has found its way into Mac

Faraday's hands and he can't resist the urge to delve into the case.

In Pittsburgh, Pennsylvania, former JAG lawyer Joshua Thornton agrees to do a favor for the last person he would ever expect to do a favor—a convicted serial killer. The Favor: Solve the one murder wrongly attributed to him.

In *Shades of Murder*, author Lauren Carr tackles the task of penning two mysteries with two detectives in two different settings and bringing them together to find one killer. "What can I say?" Carr says. "I love mysteries and mystery writing. Two cases are twice the fun."

In her fifth mystery, Lauren Car brings back her first literary detective while introducing a new one. In Shades of Murder, Joshua Thornton teams up with Cameron Gates, a spunky detective who has reason to believe the young woman listed as the victim of a serial killer was murdered by a copycat. Together, Joshua and Cameron set out to light a flame under the cold case only to find that someone behind the scenes wants the case to remain cold, and is willing to kill to keep it that way.

# The Joshua Thornton Mysteries

## A SMALL CASE OF MURDER

*Independent Publisher Book Award Finalist!*

*A Small Case of Murder is a GRAND case of murder. Following a style, reminiscent of that of Lisa Scottoline, and David Rosenfelt, Lauren Carr in her debut novel A Small Case of Murder, delivers a powerful and strong detective- legal thriller that has all the makings of a Hollywood movie.*

**New Mystery Reader**

*Carr weaves an extraordinary story that is gripping and crafted at the highest level to entertain the reader with its touch familial centerpiece amidst evil and chaos.*

**Midwest Book Reviews**

*A Small Case of Murder* is set in the quaint West Virginia town of Chester, where everyone knows everyone, and there is never a secret that someone doesn't know. In such an intimate town, how many suspicious deaths can be left unquestioned?

Following his wife's death, Joshua Thornton leaves a promising career in the U. S. Navy's JAG division to move across country with his five children into his ancestral home. While clearing out the attic they find a letter written to their grandmother postmarked 34 years ago.

In the letter, Lulu Jefferson wrote "*...Remember that dead body we found in the Bosley barn?...I saw him today...I went to talk to the reverend and there was his picture on the wall.*" *What dead* *body?* His interest piqued, Joshua asks about Lulu and finds that in 1970 she died on the same day that she penned the letter implicating the pastor in an unreported murder. There is much more to this story than a 34-year-old letter. It's a 34-year-old mystery!

Today, a double murder has the whole town under a microscope. The state attorney general appoints Joshua special prosecutor to solve the crimes. In a small town where gossip flies as swiftly as a spring breeze, it is impossible to know who to trust. Asking simple questions about events long ago could prove to be deadly for Joshua and his family.

## A Reunion to Die For

*Lauren Carr writes with a flair that will not only keep you reading but also make you glad you didn't graduate with this class!*

**Romance Reviews Today**

High school cheerleader Tricia Wheeler didn't make it to her graduation because a bullet went through her heart and killed her.

Twenty years later, a journalist is investigating Tricia's supposed suicide for a book. Suddenly, a second cheerleader is dead and the body count in the small West Virginia town continues to rise.

For Joshua Thornton, the case is personal. The reopening of the Wheeler case stirs up memories and feelings for a girl who died without knowing his true feelings for her. Now, the newly-elected prosecutor is challenged to use everything he's got to find out what had really happened to Tricia and stop the killing.

COMING SPRING 2013!

# BLAST FROM THE PAST

***A Mac Faraday Mystery!***

Made in the USA
Lexington, KY
18 December 2012